THE DOWNFALL OF DANIELLE

Johnny pulled her towards him and held her in his strong arms. The water from his body wet her clothes but she didn't care. He moved his face towards her, his eyes never leaving hers, and Danielle felt his lips on hers for the first time. He pushed his tongue between them and she accepted it into her mouth and ran her tongue across it. She moved closer and felt him pressing into her belly. He tugged her blouse out of the waistband of her skirt and began fumbling with the buttons. She wished he would just rip it off her body so that she could feel his hard hands on her naked flesh. Eventually he slid it off her shoulders. He found the zip at the back of her skirt and pulled it down, then pushed the garment over her hips so that it fell to the floor and she stepped out of it. He stood back and looked at her. 'Beautiful,' he breathed.

Also by Holly Delatour

What Katy Dunn Did

The Downfall of Danielle

Holly Delatour

HEADLINE
DELTA

The Downfall of
Danielle

1

Danielle Morgan drove her white Volkswagen Golf GTI convertible through the lanes of Surrey with the top down, the wind flying through her mane of long blonde hair, and Simply Red playing on the stereo.

At twenty-five years old she was stunning to look at, and knew it. She stood five foot nine in flat heels, with a perfect thirty-six, twenty-four, thirty-six inch figure. Her breasts were firm and upright, her waist was in perfect proportion to them and flared out into the roundness of her hips and bottom, and her long, shapely legs.

Her heart-shaped face was beautiful. She had a pair of cornflower blue, bedroom eyes, a pert nose, full red lips and cheeks that dimpled when she smiled, which she did often. But not so often lately.

She was heading towards Southampton, where she was due to meet her husband, Nigel, a sales director for a leading electronics company. They had planned to have dinner with one of the salesmen on his team and his wife. Danielle had decided to drive down from London during the morning, taking the pretty way. She wanted to check into the hotel where she was to spend the night with Nigel early, so that she could look round the town and go shopping before her husband arrived from a sales conference he had been attending in the West Country. He wasn't due to arrive until six, so she had all day.

She passed through the village of Drenham at just before noon, took a right onto the B7658, heading south, when disaster struck.

As she crossed a hump-backed bridge, just after passing a pub called The Traveller's Rest, she noticed that the needle on the temperature gauge in the Golf was on the red. Then, as she slowed to make another turn, wisps of steam appeared from inside the bonnet of the car.

'Damn,' she said, slowed and pulled onto the side of the road, stopped the car and turned off the engine. She heard the sound of bubbling water above the music coming from the speakers and the front of the car disappeared in a cloud of yet more steam.

She waited for a minute or two and tried to start the car again. It wouldn't. She ground the starter until she was afraid that the battery would go flat. Then she gave up, sat back in her seat and hit the steering wheel in exasperation.

'Damn,' she said again, leaning over to open the glove compartment. She found the AA book, looked up the local emergency number, and called it on her car phone. It was answered almost immediately. She gave her AA number and location and told the operator that her car had over-heated and wouldn't start.

'Hold on madam,' said the voice.

He came back onto the line almost immediately. 'You're in luck,' he said. 'We have a contract with a local garage in Drenham. They're on their way. Stay put. They'll be with you in a few minutes.'

'Thank you,' said Danielle, and replaced the receiver on the hook.

She wondered if she should walk back to the pub, looked over the side of the car, pulled a face in distaste, and decided not to. On one side was a ditch full of water, on the other, the road was coated with mud from farm vehicles. She looked down at the fine leather of her high-heeled shoes, and decided that she would stay exactly where she was until help arrived.

It didn't take long. Within ten minutes she saw the orange emergency light of a huge tow-truck mount the hump of the bridge behind her. It slowed to pass her, then pulled in front of the tiny Volkswagen.

The driver's door of the truck opened and a huge man jumped down onto the muddy tarmac of the road. He was tall, with short, cropped, dark hair and a very tanned, muscular body, and was dressed in a sweat-stained grey vest, very tight blue jeans that hugged his bottom and crotch – revealing a hard lump inside the fly – and brown, lace-up boots. His face was weather-beaten and handsome and he looked to be about forty. He smiled at Danielle as he made his way up to her door.

'Got some trouble, ma'am?' he asked as he reached her.

'She just packed up on me. There was a lot of steam,' said Danielle. 'Thank you for being so quick.' She smiled and saw his brown eyes watching her.

'No trouble. We're just up the road,' said the driver, and smiled back. 'Would you open the bonnet catch please?'

She did as he asked and he stuck his head into the engine compartment for a minute. Then he stood up, slammed the bonnet and said, 'Thermostat. I'll have to take you back to the garage.'

'Will it take long,' she asked. 'I'm due in Southampton later to meet my husband.'

The driver looked at his watch. 'No problem. The spares shop doesn't close for lunch 'til one thirty. I'll be there and back, and you'll be on you way in no time. Fitting a new 'stat takes no time.'

'That's very kind of you,' said Danielle with another smile. 'It's my job, ma'am,' he said. 'Do you want to sit in the cab while I hook your motor up to the truck.'

'The road's very muddy,' said Danielle. 'And my shoes aren't exactly designed for a cross country walk.'

'No problem,' said the driver. He walked round to Danielle's door again, opened it and picked her out of the driver's seat as if she weighed no more than a feather.

Danielle had never been so surprised in all her life. She wanted to protest, but the truck driver did it so casually that she didn't have time. Before she knew what was happening, she was in his arms and he was carrying her to the tow-truck.

For her journey to Southampton she had worn matching white underwear: an underwired, low-cut bra; tiny lace panties, with no side panels and just a thin strip of elastic between the twin triangles of material that made up the garment; and a lace suspender belt with charcoal nylons. On top she had worn a simple white blouse and a short black skirt, the matching jacket to which lay on the passenger seat of the VW. As she was carried to the truck she could feel that the skirt had ridden up, and the driver's bare arms were holding the naked flesh above her stocking tops. She was sure that he was looking down into her cleavage and she blushed to the roots of her hair.

She knew she should have been outraged at the treatment, but in fact she rather enjoyed it. She liked the feel of strength and warmth in his powerful, muscular arms, the thickness of his chest, and the male smell of motor oil and sweat on his body, and she leaned back into it as he carried her. 'Apologies, ma'am,' he said as he went. 'But it's easier this way. I don't want you in the car whilst I put it on the hoist.'

He boosted her up through the open door of the truck. As he did so, his hand slid almost up to her panties, but he seemed not to notice – which Danielle found most unflattering.

'Won't be long, love,' he said. 'Slide over, and I'll be with you in a minute.'

This wasn't the way AA men behaved or spoke to customers in London, Danielle knew, but she did as she was told, sliding over to the passenger side of the truck, and watched him hitch her little car onto the truck in the mirror on the door.

As she sat on the wide, bench seat, she could feel a strange hot tickling between her legs at the sight of the truck driver working, and at the memory of how it had felt when he'd been carrying her. She admired his body as he chained the VW onto the back of the truck. It was a lot different from Nigel's skinny white body. Not that she would have cared how skinny her husband was, if, by word or deed he had once given her the feeling in their five years of marriage that the truck driver had given her in thirty seconds.

She felt sad at the thought. She hated being disloyal to Nigel, but lately, and after such a relatively short time being his wife, she felt that most of any magic there had ever been between them had vanished from their marriage.

I was too young, she thought. Too inexperienced. A virgin. A twenty-year-old virgin getting married to a man with hardly any more experience than I'd had. In 1988. Ridiculous. From what she saw in magazines and on television, being a virgin at twenty was almost unheard of in these liberated times. But she had been, and that was a fact. And now she bitterly regretted it.

And she'd been faithful to Nigel throughout their marriage. Not that she hadn't had offers. God, there'd been dozens. If not scores. Every man she met it seemed. From the window cleaner who called at their house once a fortnight, to old Man Guggenheim, Nigel's boss. They all took every opportunity they could find to paw at her and leer dirty words into her ears. But despite every offer of drinks, dinner, presents, holidays, jewels, God knows what, that had come her way, she had remained faithful to her husband. But it had been hard at times to resist the offers. After all, she was a red blooded woman who wanted all the things that red blooded women wanted. Including a decent sex life.

And suddenly, looking at the breakdown truck driver as he finished securing her car onto his vehicle, she was desperately sorry that she had.

2

The driver, who introduced himself as Dave Harvey when he climbed behind the steering wheel, turned the truck round in the entrance to a field and headed back to Drenham. He turned off just before the village, bounced the vehicle down a rutted lane, and into an area fenced off with chainlink that contained a large shed and a silver caravan which had been jacked up onto blocks.

In front of the shed were three or four cars of medium age. There was a yellow 'AA Approved' sign tacked to the side of the building.

'I'll go and get the part I need,' said Dave. 'You'd better wait in the van.'

Danielle looked down at the filthy, mud spattered concrete where he'd stopped the truck.

'Are you going to carry me again?' she asked, and before the words were out of her mouth she reddened again.

What's come over me she thought. This man *is* having an affect on me.

'If you want,' said Dave. 'It is pretty dirty out there, and we don't want to mess up your nice clean shoes.'

He got out of the truck, walked around to Danielle's side and opened the door. Danielle stepped down onto the running board and Dave picked her up again and walked her over to the caravan.

She thrilled as he carried her and longed to lean her head onto his broad shoulder as he did so, but resisted the temptation and put one arm over it instead. She could feel the muscles of his chest against her breast, and it suddenly felt heavy and hot and too big for its skin. His hand was under her thighs again, and she knew that he must be able to feel the fasteners of her suspenders at the top of her stockings. Her vagina began to lubricate at the thought.

When he got to the caravan he kicked at the door. 'Johnny,' he shouted. 'Open up.'

Danielle looked into Dave's face in surprise, and was suddenly very aware of how things must look. She hadn't expected anyone else to be at the garage.

'You can put me down now,' she said. 'I'll be all right.'

Dave smiled at her alarm. 'Don't worry,' he said. 'It's only me baby brother.'

Danielle thought that the man in his late twenties who opened the door to the caravan could hardly be described as a baby. He stood about six foot two in his bare feet and had to stoop in the doorway.

He was wearing just a pair of ragged boxer shorts and his physique almost took Danielle's breath away. Two of them, she thought. I envy the young girls who live in this village.

'This is Mrs Morgan,' said Dave. 'She's got her pretty shoes on, and didn't want to get them wet. Here, you take her.' And he casually tossed Danielle into his brother's arms, who accepted the load with all the panache of someone who gets handed beautiful blondes every day of his life.

The way she was being treated, and the off-hand fashion in which the men passed her between them, like a chattel, made Danielle feel even more feminine and excited, if that were possible. As Johnny took her from his brother, her skirt slid right up over her stocking tops, exposing several inches of creamy skin made even whiter by the contrast of the black material and the dark grey band at the top of her nylons. She didn't even try to cover herself, allowing the pair of them to feast their eyes on her for as long as they wished. Johnny stood holding her inside the doorway of the caravan for half a minute and Danielle luxuriated in being the object of attention of two pairs of lustful, dark eyes.

'Make her a brew,' said Dave. 'I'll take the Ford down the factors. I won't be long. Take care of her, do you hear?' And he turned and walked away towards the garage without another word.

The young man grunted and put Danielle's feet on the floor of the caravan. Then he walked over to the gas stove without a backward glance.

Danielle adjusted her clothing and looked round the interior of the dwelling. It was primitively furnished, with just two unmade beds, a fold-away table, a small fridge, the stove, and three wooden boxes that had once held bottles of beer piled up in one corner for storage. Inside the caravan, the air smelled of oil and sweat and maleness, just like Dave's body had.

'Sit down,' said Johnny. 'Do you take sugar?'

'Yes. Where?'

'On the bed. How many?'

'Just half a spoonful,' she said, and sat on the bed where the male smell was stronger and more potent. As she sat, she crossed her long legs, and her skirt slid up her thighs to her stocking tops again. As she was about to pull it down, she hesitated, and left it where it was.

'Your brother's very strong,' she said.

'Yeah,' Johnny replied.

'And so are you.'

He shrugged, and all the muscles on his back moved under the skin in a very appealing way.

When he'd brewed up, he brought Danielle a mug of hot strong tea. She saw by his look that he'd noticed the way she was sitting.

He walked back to the stove, collected his own mug and hitched himself onto the edge of the table. As he did so, his shorts tightened around his groin, and Danielle was sure she could see the outline of his dark pubic hair and the shape of his genitals beneath the thin material.

'What's your name?' he asked.

'Mrs Morgan.'

'Your first name.'

'Danielle.'

'That's nice.'

'Thank you,' she said and smiled.

'Are you from London?'

She nodded and re-crossed her legs slowly, so that he would have another good view of her naked thighs.

'Down on holiday?' he asked, as if he hadn't noticed, but she knew that he had.

'I'm meeting my husband in Southampton later.'

'How long have you been married?'

'Five years.'

'Any kids?'

She shook her head.

'He's not doing a very good job is he?' said Johnny insolently. 'I'm going to take a shower.' And he put his cup down, slid off the table and walked past Danielle to the back of the caravan.

Cheeky sod, she thought, but the inside of her panties were still soaking, and stuck to her pubic hair like glue.

She heard the sound of running water and looked round. Through the doorless gap to the rear of the caravan she could see a dusty old mirror on the wall, and in the mirror she could see straight into the shower compartment. It was nothing more than a three-sided plastic box, with the fourth side completely open. Johnny was standing facing the mirror soaping his hair under a thin stream of water. From where she was sitting she could see his cock clearly. She thought it was the most beautiful thing she'd ever seen. It was darker than the rest of his body and nestled neatly in his pubic hair, and the balls behind it looked round and hard.

Danielle felt herself lubricating again; a hot rush of liquid between her legs like she could never remember experiencing before, even in the grip of her wildest fantasies.

She could hardly tear her eyes away, but after a minute or so she turned to the front again.

Eventually the sound of water ceased, and a few seconds later Johnny said, 'Can you pass me that towel? The one on top of the fridge.'

Danielle got to her feet without looking round and walked over and picked up the towel. When she turned round he was standing in the doorway, naked. He looked like a god, with his dark hair slicked back, and drops of water all over his body. His cock was halfway erect and poked out lazily from his bush of pubic hair. She suddenly wanted to see it totally erect, and kiss it, and feel it poking inside her.

'Hurry up,' he said. 'I'm dripping.'

She walked towards him and he turned away to expose the most beautiful pair of bare buttocks that Danielle had ever seen. 'Dry my back,' he ordered.

Once again she did as she was told and began to rub his shoulders and back with the thin material of the towel. Then, without being asked, she moved the towel down and began to rub the hard muscles of his bottom.

He turned round and took the towel from her hands and dropped it on the floor. Now his cock was totally erect, and Danielle drew a sharp breath when she saw the size of it. It was huge and fat, ridged with veins, and the knob was blue with blood. It made her husband's look tiny by comparison, and she wondered if she could accommodate it. But she knew she'd happily die trying.

Johnny pulled her towards him and held her in his strong arms. The water from his body wet her clothes, but she didn't care. He moved his face towards her, his eyes never leaving hers, and Danielle felt his lips on hers for the first time. He pushed his tongue between them, and she accepted it into her mouth and ran her own tongue across it. She moved closer and felt his prick pressing into her belly. He tugged her blouse out of the waistband of her skirt and began fumbling with the buttons. She wished he would just rip it off her body so that she could feel his hard hands on her naked flesh. Eventually he slid it off her shoulders. He found the zip at the back of her skirt and pulled it down, then pushed the garment over her hips so that it fell to the floor and she stepped out of it. He stood back and looked at her. 'Beautiful,' he breathed.

'So are you,' she said.

He reached round and unfastened the catch at the back of her bra, pulling the straps off her shoulders to allow her breasts freedom. She stood in front of him and smiled as he looked down at them. They stood proud and the nipples were hard and engorged with blood.

He led her over to one of the beds and laid her down on the crumpled bedclothes, then joined her. His mouth went straight to the nipple on her left breast. He kissed, sucked and teased it with his mouth and tongue, until it was red and sore looking, and she felt every touch deep inside her belly.

She found his massive cock with her hand and began to stroke it almost shyly.

He moved his mouth back onto hers and they kissed again; long, passionate kisses that left Danielle breathless; and wanting more. He kissed her eyes and ears and neck, before returning his mouth to her breasts again, and then kissed her all the way down to the elastic at the top of her knickers. As his mouth got closer to her cunt, Danielle began to tremble with desire.

'Fuck me,' she begged. 'Please fuck me. I need you.'

She saw him grin, and he gently eased her brief panties down over her hips and legs until she could kick them free. She opened her legs wide and he looked at the blonde hair that covered her pubis. He slid the fingers of one hand into the curls and she trembled even more at his touch. Each caress was like fire between her legs and she could hardly stop herself from begging for his prick again.

His fingertips found the soaking lips of her cunt and gently caressed the delicate membrane between her legs.

She opened for him like a flower in the sunshine and she felt him enter her with first one, then two, then three fingers, and she began to wank his cock with her hand.

She couldn't bear the pleasure she was feeling a moment

longer. 'Please,' she cried. 'Before your brother gets back.'

'Suck my cock first,' he said. She did so gladly. She went down on him, and wet the tip with her tongue before sliding it between her lips. It felt huge inside her mouth, but she bravely pushed it up until it touched the back of her throat. Then she slid it out again and began to suck the end like it was a lollipop. She looked up at him and winked, and he pulled her up and kissed her again.

'Please,' she said again, and he mounted her with one smooth movement. She felt the knob of his cock between her legs as he deftly guided it into her wet slit and pushed it up the length of her.

As the huge weapon slid up towards her womb, she felt herself open even more to accommodate the massive size of it and she called out his name in sheer pleasure.

He began to move inside her. In and out he pushed his cock, and she could hear her juices squelching on it as he went.

He began to move faster and faster, and every movement sent a thrill of ecstasy through her entire body. She began to move with him until their bodies were beating at each other like twin hammers. Danielle felt the ecstasy increase, until she could bear it no longer, and she sank her fingernails into his back and screamed out his name over and over again as she orgasmed onto his mighty cock.

She heard him calling her name also and he pumped harder and harder until he stiffened over her and shot his load into her cunt like boiling water from the spout of a kettle.

He dropped onto her body and lay still, with only the beating of his heart against hers proving that she hadn't fucked him to death.

After a minute or so he looked up into her face and smiled a beatific smile. 'That was great,' he said. 'You're wonderful.'

'You too,' she said back. 'I never knew sex could be like that.'

He kissed her, and climbed gently off her body, pulling his wet prick from inside her. Then he went into the back of the caravan again, and reappeared wearing a check shirt, filthy jeans, and a pair of black leather boots without laces. He walked to the door of the caravan and looked out. As he did so, they both heard the sound of a car engine.

'Dave's here,' he said.

Danielle lay back on the bed. She knew she should get up and dress, but she wanted to see Dave again – and she wanted him to see her as she was. Naked after sex, except for stockings and suspenders, with his brother's come leaking out from between her legs. 'Will he mind?' she asked.

Johnny looked over at her and winked. 'Mind,' he said. 'Not him. He's very broadminded is Dave.'

3

The car drew up outside and Danielle heard the door slam. She pulled the edge of the sheet on the bed where she was lying across her naked maidenhead. Johnny turned, smiled and winked, and Dave came into the caravan. He looked over at Danielle and smiled too. 'Been having fun, you two?' he asked.

'Sure, big brother,' said Johnny.

'I can't leave you alone for a minute, can I?' said Dave to his brother, and held up a plastic bag he was carrying. 'Inside there is the replacement thermostat for Mrs Morgan's Golf. You put it in. I'm going to be busy for a while.'

Danielle felt a thrill run through her at his words. Did he mean to fuck her too? she thought. Not that she minded. Suddenly for some reason, all her previous moral code seemed to have flown out of the window of the airless caravan in which she lay.

'OK, Dave,' said Johnny. 'Anything you say.' And he took the bag, winked at Danielle again, and walked out of the door.

Dave Harvey went to the fridge and took out a can of beer. 'Want one?' he asked.

'Can I have a drop of yours?' said Danielle.

'Course.' He popped the top, and took a long drink

before taking the tin over to her, and putting it in her hand.

She took a sip, and saw that he was running his eyes all over her body. She lay with her arm behind her head and looked him up and down too. She saw that the lump in his jeans was bigger than she remembered it and knew that he was getting excited looking at her.

He took the can back and finished the beer with one swallow. Then he tugged his vest over his head, bent down and took off his boots and socks, undid his belt, and unbuttoned the fly of his jeans.

He pushed them down his legs, and Danielle saw that he was naked underneath. His cock popped upright, and she realised that if anything it was bigger and more beautiful than his brother's.

He leant over and flipped the edge of the sheet off her pubis. Danielle opened her legs so that he could see the wetness in her hair, and on the tops of her thighs.

'Did you enjoy being fucked by my little brother?' he asked as he sat on the edge of the bed and began to stroke her nylon-clad legs.

She nodded.

'And you a married woman too. Have you no shame?'

She shook her head.

'Do you want some more?'

She nodded again.

'Come here and kiss me then,' he said.

She was in his arms in a second, nestling herself up against the muscles of his mighty chest and lifting her face to be kissed.

He obliged wonderfully. His mouth covered hers and they were soon exchanging the longest, most passionate kisses that Danielle could ever remember experiencing.

Dave's hand roamed her body as if he owned it. He stroked and teased and tickled and caressed her all over. Her nipples were soon hard and red again, and he dropped his head to cover them in tiny, sweet kisses that almost drove her crazy, and lubricated the insides of her cunt once more with hot, creamy secretions, making it even wetter and more welcoming.

As her pussy opened in anticipation of the treat it had in store, Danielle reached for Dave's manhood. It was huge and hot in her hand and she pulled the foreskin back to expose the knob of it, which felt as big as a tennis ball in her tiny hand.

She licked her fingers and massaged the end with the wetness on them, and the skin gleamed in the dim light inside the caravan.

David rolled her over and began to kiss her thighs above her stocking tops, playing with the straps of her suspenders, snapping them against her skin. He moved his face into the cleft of her bottom, pulled her buttocks apart, and found her arsehole with his tongue. She moaned in pleasure as it flicked over the opening, giving her feelings of pleasure that she had never before got from sex.

She felt Dave's weight bearing down on her legs and she wanted him to squash her so hard that she would melt into the bedclothes and be with him forever.

All at once she felt him roll her onto her back again, and she bent her knees and opened her legs in anticipation of what was to come. He climbed between them and, for the second time that day, she felt a huge rod of maleness pushing at the most private entrance to her body. Her cunt, already stretched from Johnny's prick, accepted Dave's easily, and using the mixture of her wetness and Johnny's come, it slid effortlessly along the length of her vagina, and into the entrance to her womb. She could feel the whole length of it stretching her insides, and revelled in the feeling of wholeness that it gave her.

He began to move on top of her and she could feel her cunt skin stroking his prick to a climax.

He moved slowly at first, looking down at her, then kissing her face, to which she responded with kisses of her own. She put her heels onto his calves, moved them up to his thighs and finally wrapped them round his waist, in order to better feel the movement of his cock in her box. He began to move faster, and she anticipated him shooting his load into her cunt – already swimming with seed – when he pulled out and rolled her onto her front again.

He dipped his fingers into her pussy and spread the glop he found there up the crack of her arse to the hole again. Then, using it as lubricant, he pushed his forefinger inside. Danielle began to protest, but he shushed her, working his finger in up to the knuckle. Danielle had never had anything like it done to her before. She was a well brought up girl, married to a well brought up man, and such people didn't do things like this. She couldn't think why. The sensation was wonderful. Unlike any she'd ever felt. He pushed in a second finger and a third, widening the hole all the time. Then he mounted her from behind. She didn't believe what was happening as he pushed the huge knob of his cock into her anus.

'It won't fit,' she cried, as a sharp pain shot through her. She felt him bearing down on her slowly, and slowly her arsehole opened to allow his cock entry into her back passage. The pain was intense for another few seconds, and then, when she thought she could bear it no more, it changed to a beautiful heat that ran up through her belly to her breasts. He kept pushing his cock into her until it was in up to the hilt. Then he began fucking her up the arse. As he moved, the heat increased, and she knew that her orgasm was imminent. Instead of telling him to stop, she goaded him to fuck her harder and faster, which he did, until she screamed so loudly with pleasure as she came, that she thought the whole world would hear. Dave pounded her buttocks half a dozen more times, until he too climaxed, shooting hot spunk into her bottom until she thought she would die with the ecstasy of it.

4

Danielle and Dave lay together for half an hour, half asleep, half awake, languidly stroking each other as the afternoon got older.

At about two-thirty, Johnny rapped on the side of the caravan. 'Job done,' he shouted.

Danielle looked at Dave and said, 'I'd better get dressed. I've got to get down to Southampton.'

'Do you have to go?' he asked.

'My husband's expecting me.'

He shrugged ruefully, eased himself over and kissed her hard and long. Then he climbed off the bed and began to put on his clothes. She watched him, and wished that she could stay and sample the delights of his and his brother's lovemaking again. When Dave was dressed, he said, 'I'd better check your car.' He kissed her again and went outside.

Danielle got up too. She felt like she'd been beaten with a big stick. Two big sticks, she thought naughtily. She was stiff and sleepy, and her stockings were ripped and laddered. She took them and her suspender belt off, then pulled on her panties, blouse, skirt, and pushed her feet into her shoes. She went to the mirror in the back of the caravan to check out the damage. Surprisingly she looked pretty normal. Not at all like she thought a married woman who'd just sampled the carnal delights she had would look. She found a comb on a shelf by the shower stall and ran it through her thick hair, then went to the door of the caravan holding her stockings, suspender belt and bra in her hand.

Dave was sitting in her car, with the engine running, and when he saw her he ran it up to where she was standing. Johnny came and joined them.

'How much do I owe you?' she asked.

'On the house,' said Dave, as he got out of the car.

'No, I must.'

He shook his head. 'You're a friend,' he said. 'And here we don't charge friends.'

'Thanks,' she said shyly. 'Thanks for everything.' And all three of them laughed.

Dave said. 'Want to be carried?'

She nodded, and he lifted her off the step of the caravan and placed her gently behind the wheel of the Golf.

'Got to keep your shoes clean,' he said.

Self-consciously she stuffed her underwear into the glove compartment. 'I'd better be going,' she said.

'Anytime you're passing,' said Johnny, 'come and visit a pair of lonely bachelors. You're always welcome.'

'I bet you're not that lonely,' she replied, engaged gear, and pulled away with a wave. 'But I'll take you up on the invitation someday,' she shouted back, as she drove out of the garage compound in the direction of the coast again.

She pulled into the parking area of the Southampton Holiday Inn at just after four o'clock. She stuffed the incriminating evidence from the glove compartment into her handbag, collected her small suitcase from the boot, checked in and, shopping and sightseeing forgotten, she went straight to her room and ran a bath. She unpacked and undressed, hiding all the clothes she had worn that day back in the case. Better not let Nigel see that lot, she thought, and went back into the bathroom. She slid into the bubble-filled water and smiled to herself as she caressed her body where her two lovers had caressed it earlier.

You're such a naughty girl, she thought, as she washed their semen out of her cunt. But such a satisfied one.

She lay in the hot water for more than an hour before getting out and towelling herself down. When she looked in the full-length mirror on the wall there was no sign of what she'd been up to earlier, and she winked at her own reflection. She washed her hair, and as she was drying it the telephone rang.

It was Nigel.

'Darling,' he said. 'Bad news. I'm stuck in a meeting. I don't know when I'll be able to get away and it'll be hours before I'm with you.'

'Oh, Nigel,' she said.

'I know it's a nuisance, but it can't be helped.'

'What am I going to do?'

'Well you know Roger Clinton and his wife are meeting us for dinner. Will you play hostess? And I'll get there in time for coffee. They're a lovely couple. They've always entertained me when I've been on that part of the coast on business. I don't want to put them off. Say you will.'

'What will we talk about?'

'You'll think of something. Don't worry. You'll charm the pants off the pair of them.'

Bad choice of expression thought Danielle, after what had happened on the way down.

'All right, darling,' she agreed. 'But do try and get here as quickly as you can.'

'I will, I promise,' he said. 'Look I'd better get back. Love you,' and he put down the phone.

'Love you too,' she said to dead air, and replaced the receiver at her end too.

'Damn it,' she thought as she stood up and finished drying her hair. Stuck in a hotel restaurant with two people I've never met before, talking about oil all evening. What a bore.

Still, I'm as much married to his job as to him, so I'd better put on my best dress and my bravest face and enter the battle unafraid.

She looked at her watch. Five-thirty. Plenty of time, she thought. I think I'll have a drink in the bar first. A little Dutch courage never did anyone any harm.

She went to the wardrobe to get her dress. It was black, low cut and short. David loved her in it. She hoped that Mr and Mrs Clinton would too.

She found her underwear and stockings in the drawer where she'd put them. It was going to be an all-black night tonight – whatever way you looked at it, she thought.

She fastened a black suspender belt around her waist, pulled on sheer, seamed black stockings and fastened then tightly. Then she put on a black net, half bra, and the tiniest pair of black net panties that matched it. She went back into the bathroom and admired her reflection again. Not bad, she thought. I bet I could get a few pulses racing in this outfit tonight if I tried. She went back to the bedroom and applied her make-up. When satisfied, she stepped into the dress and fastened the zipper. Finally she put on a pair of very high-heeled black leather court shoes, got her black leather handbag, left the room, locking it behind her, and went down to the bar.

On the way, she stopped at the desk and told the receptionist that if a Mr and Mrs Clinton asked for her, she'd be in the cocktail bar.

Being quite early, the bar was almost empty when Danielle walked in. She went up to the counter and a good looking young barman sped to serve her.

Points to me, she thought.

'Good evening madam,' he said. 'What's your pleasure tonight?'

She didn't miss the double meaning of his question. What is happening to me? she thought.

'A large gin and tonic,' she replied.

'Coming right up. Are you a resident?'

'Yes.'

'Shall I put it on your bill?'

'Please.'

'Room number?'

Danielle showed him her key.

Within seconds he placed the drink on a mat in front of her and waited for her to taste it, as if the future of nations hung on her verdict.

'Very nice,' she said.

'We're here to serve you,' replied the barman.

'I think I'll sit down,' said Danielle. 'I'm expecting guests.'

'Make yourself comfortable. If there's anything else you require. Just ask. Anything at all.'

Danielle didn't miss the double meaning in that either.

'I will,' she replied, and took her drink to a table in the corner of the bar where she had a good view of the doorway and the rest of the room.

At one end of the bar itself, a handsome, dark-haired man was sitting alone. He'd noticed Danielle's entrance and had listened to her short conversation with the barman. Now he sat looking at her in the mirror at the back of the bar.

She's stunning, he thought. Quite stunning. I wonder who her guests are, and why she's here on her own.

There was only one way to find out, he decided, and took his drink to the table next to where Danielle was sitting.

'Good evening,' he said.

'Good evening,' replied Danielle, looking up in surprise.

My, but he's good looking, she thought, feeling the now familiar tickling between her legs, and her nipples hardened and rubbed against the net of her bra in a most delicious way.

'Forgive me, but I couldn't help noticing you. Are you all alone?' asked the man.

'Temporarily. I'm waiting for some dinner guests. And my husband is arriving later.'

'He's a very lucky man if I may say so,' said the stranger.

'You may, and thank you,' said Danielle, feeling herself colour slightly at the compliment.

The stranger noticed the blush on her peaches-and-cream complexion and felt himself react to it.

'My name is Laurence,' he said. 'Laurence Stark. Forgive me for intruding. If you wish I shall leave.'

'Not at all,' said Danielle. 'My guests aren't due until seven thirty. It would be nice to have someone to talk to.'

'May I join you?' asked Laurence.

'Of course.'

The man picked up his drink and moved to Danielle's table. 'But I'm afraid you have an advantage on me.'

Danielle looked puzzled, then realised what he was talking about. 'I'm sorry,' she said. 'I'm Danielle. Danielle Morgan.'

'Danielle,' said Laurence. 'What a beautiful name.' He shook her hand, and pulled up a chair next to hers. 'So what are you doing in Southampton? Apart from having dinner and meeting your husband of course.'

'That's all,' replied Danielle. 'He's been away on business and we thought it would make a pleasant change to meet in a hotel. He was due to entertain one of his salesmen tonight, and we thought we'd kill two birds with one stone.'

'Excellent,' said Laurence. 'But you said "was".'

Danielle explained what had happened, and they chatted together for another hour or more. Laurence bought Danielle another large gin and the liquor began to loosen her tongue. She confided that her marriage was not a particularly happy one and he commiserated with her.

At seven-fifteen he excused himself. 'I have an appointment of my own,' he explained. 'A business appointment. This has been a most charming meeting. I'm sorry to abandon you. But your guests should be here soon. I hope we meet again.'

'So do I,' said Danielle, who was becoming more and more attracted to him. 'Good night.'

'Good night,' said Laurence. As he left the room he found himself thinking that if they didn't meet again, he wasn't the Laurence Stark he knew himself to be.

* * *

Roger Clinton arrived alone at seven-forty-five. He burst into the bar, looked round and came straight over to Danielle.

'Mrs Morgan?' he asked.

'Yes.'

'I thought it must be you. I am sorry for being late. It's been a hell of an evening. Our baby-sitter let us down at the last moment and we couldn't get another at such short notice. So I had to leave Anne behind to look after the sprog. She was so disappointed. She was really looking forward to tonight. Please accept our apologies. We wouldn't have had this happen for the world.'

Roger Clinton was about Danielle's own age. He was above medium height, with a broad, athletic frame, and not bad looking, she thought. His crisp dark hair was cut short, and he was wearing a dark suit and a white shirt with a colourful tie.

'Don't worry,' said Danielle. 'It's not a problem. Sit down and have a drink. You look like you need one.'

'I do,' said Roger, and slumped into the chair recently vacated by Laurence.

Danielle caught the eye of the barman who had served her earlier and he rushed across at her summons.

'Madam,' he said. He had not missed Laurence joining her. And now another man was at her table. He didn't blame them for buzzing around like flies, she was a stunner and no mistake.

'Roger?' said Danielle.

'A beer,' said Roger. 'Bottled. Anything.'

'I'll have another gin and tonic,' said Danielle.

The barman vanished.

'Where's Nigel?' asked Roger. 'Is he upstairs?'

Danielle explained for the second time what had happened to her husband.

'Lord,' said Roger. 'What a disastrous evening.'

Danielle looked at the young man sitting opposite her. 'Not at all,' she said. 'I'm here, and you're here. Let's enjoy ourselves. The company's footing the bill. We'll eat, drink and be merry.'

The barman arrived with the drinks and Roger and Danielle toasted each other.

'Why not?' said Roger. 'That's a very good idea.'

5

Danielle and Roger dined on quail's eggs, roast lamb with all the trimmings and orange sorbet. They drank pink champagne and Cointreau with their coffee. As the evening progressed, and the alcohol flowed, Danielle found herself more and more attracted to the young salesman and she knew that the feeling was mutual.

Normally, she wouldn't have done anything about the way she felt, but after her adventures on the way down to Southampton, she felt unusually bold.

At about ten o'clock they ordered more coffee and liqueurs to be served in the lounge. Danielle instructed the waiter, that if her husband arrived he was to be told where they were.

The lounge was deserted and they sat in the darkest corner, next to each other on a velvet chesterfield that faced its twin across a coffee table. The little enclave formed by the chairs made it almost impossible for anyone to see them, and that suited her down to the ground.

Just imagine what Nigel will think if he comes in, she thought. And serve him jolly well right too. It's about time he bucked his ideas up.

After the waiter had poured the coffee and left, Roger and Danielle raised their glasses and toasted each other.

'Cheers,' he said.

'Cheers,' she replied.

'Well I must say, you rescued what could have been a terrible evening,' said Roger.

'Not alone,' she countered. 'It was as much your doing as mine.'

'I haven't had such fun for years,' he went on. 'Or dined with such a charming companion.'

'You shouldn't flirt with your boss's wife,' said Danielle, with a smile.

'Is that what I'm doing? I do apologise,' he said.

'No. Don't stop. I like it.'

He smiled and took the glass from her hand and placed it, with his, on the low table in front of them.

'Is that right?' he asked huskily.

Danielle just smiled again in reply.

Roger reached for her and she slid into his arms as if she were oiled. He kissed her lips gently and she responded by opening her mouth to him in surrender.

They kissed for several minutes before Roger put his hand on Danielle's knee and slid it up towards her crotch. He found her suspenders, and the bare skin of her thigh. She opened her legs slightly to allow him access to the silken skin there.

She shivered as his fingertips played across her naked legs, and kissed him all the harder.

He touched her breasts and once again her nipples were hard against the net of her bra. She put her hand on his thigh too, and inched it up towards what looked like a very interesting bulge in the dark wool of his trousers.

He moaned as her hand found his cock and stroked it gently.

'Don't,' he pleaded. 'You'll drive me crazy.'

'I want to see it,' said Danielle.

Roger looked round the empty room across the back of the sofa in front of him, and once sure they were still alone, he undid the zip of his pants. He fiddled around inside, and then produced the end of his very swollen, very hard knob.

By this time, Danielle was used to seeing erect penises waved about in front of her face.

'Nice,' she breathed. 'Let me kiss it.' And she leaned down and sucked up the tiny drop of moisture that was dribbling out of the hole at the end of his cock. She licked her lips greedily. 'I want more,' she said, and drew the helmet into her mouth, working her tongue and lips on it.

Roger pushed her head harder into his groin and the tip of his prick rubbed against the back of her throat. She sucked harder and harder, until she felt his whole body stiffen under her ministrations, and a thick jet of hot, creamy come fired into her mouth.

She swallowed as much as she could, the residue dribbling out from between her lips and down her chin.

Roger pulled her up and kissed her mouth wildly, sucking his own jism off her, swallowing it too.

'Fuck me,' she begged. 'I need a man so badly.'

Roger was about to tear his clothes off, when the telephone that stood on a sideboard about ten yards from where they were sitting, rang.

'Leave it,' begged Danielle.

'I can't. It must be for us. They know we're here all alone. They'll only come looking,' said Roger. He tucked himself away and went and picked up the receiver.

'Anne,' he stuttered. 'Sorry. Of course I meant to phone. I just got distracted.'

Thanks a bunch, thought Danielle. That's *your* lot lover boy. A mere distraction am I?

'Soon,' said Roger and put down the phone. 'My wife,' he said, as if he needed to. 'I'm sorry Mrs Morgan, I've got to go.'

Mrs Morgan is it now? Danielle thought angrily. You wimp.

'You'd better go then,' she said and, with a weak smile, Roger pulled up his zip, and almost ran out of the lounge.

6

When Danielle flounced into her room ten minutes later, the telephone was ringing. She picked it up as she dropped the key on the bed.

'Hello,' she said.

'Hello darling. Is that you?'

'Nigel.'

'Listen, I'm not going to be able to make it to the hotel tonight.'

'*What*?'

'I am so, so sorry.'

'So you should be,' she said. I'm as horny as hell, she thought, all alone, and dying to be fucked, and *you* can't make it. Some husband I've got.

'I had to stay to the bitter end of the meeting.'

'In the bar no doubt.'

'You know that's how it goes sometimes.'

'I know. So when will I see you?'

'Tomorrow. I'll be with you by eleven. I've spoken to the manager there, and booked an extra night. That means we can have the whole day together tomorrow.'

'All right,' said Danielle, but even as she said it, she could hear the disappointment in her voice.

'I'm sorry, darling,' said Nigel. 'I know it's a bore, but

it can't be helped. Was dinner a success?'

'You could say that. His wife couldn't make it. Baby-sitter problems,' said Danielle.

'But Roger came?'

In both senses of the word, thought Danielle.

'Yes. We had a really nice time. He's very sweet. If a bit young.'

And under his wife's thumb, she thought.

'I've always liked him,' said Nigel.

I wonder if you'd like him as much if you knew that I'd sucked his cock and swallowed his spunk, thought Danielle.

'I'll see you tomorrow, then,' she said.

'Of course you will. I'll be with you before lunch. I'll stand for the best one that we can find in Southampton. Or we'll drive out somewhere.'

'I'll look forward to it.'

'Good night then, darling. Sleep well.'

'Same to you,' she said, and hung up.

She looked at her watch. It wasn't yet midnight. She went over to the dressing-table mirror and checked her make-up.

To hell with this, she thought. I'm going to go downstairs and see if the bar is still open.

Which she did. And it was.

At that time of night, it was quite crowded, smoky and noisy. The stereo system was playing the new Genesis album, who were one of Danielle's favourite bands. She went up to the bar and the same young barman spotted her and ran up to serve her.

'Hello,' he said. 'Nice to see you again.'

'It looks like I can't keep away. You'll be thinking I'm an alcoholic.'

'Not at all. You're welcome any time. Any time at all. What can I get you?'

'I'll have a brandy I think,' said Danielle.

'Coming up.'

As the barman busied himself with the bottle and glass, Danielle looked round the room and spotted Laurence Stark at the same table they'd occupied earlier. He'd seen her too, and raised his glass in a salute.

She smiled back, collected her drink, thanked the barman and made her way across the bar. The barman watched her retreating back, and the way her bottom twitched under the tight skirt of her dress as she walked.

Lucky man, he thought of Laurence. *Very* lucky.

Laurence stood up when Danielle got to the table.

'Hello again,' he said. 'I didn't think I'd be lucky enough to see you again tonight. What happened to your guests?'

'Guest,' she said. 'The wife couldn't make it. He's been and gone.'

Or come and gone, she thought.

'Did you have a good meal?' asked Laurence.

'Yes,' replied Danielle.

And the dessert wasn't bad either, she thought, remembering the way Roger's prick had bucked inside her mouth as she sucked his sperm down her throat.

'And your husband?'

'Delayed again, I'm afraid. Business.'

'I'm so sorry.'

'I'm not. If his firm is more important than me, I have to make other arrangements.'

'Please join me then.'

'I'd like that.'

Laurence fetched a spare chair and seated Danielle close to his own.

They sat almost knee to knee and Danielle became more aware of what an attractive man he was. Suddenly her horniness returned ten-fold. She crossed her legs, and her skirt rode up her thighs and she saw that Laurence had noticed – which was exactly the way she wanted it.

'Was *your* business successful?' she asked.

'Very,' replied Laurence, who had been taken out to dinner by an attractive fifty-year-old widow. He had brought her back to his room upstairs and undressed her down to the silk and lace teddy she had worn under her dress, which he knew she wanted him to tear to shreds before making passionate love to her, as he did regularly once every three or four weeks. He remembered her cries as she climaxed on his cock with a smile, and the three hundred pounds in cash she had paid him as he put her in a taxi.

'What business is it exactly?'

'I'm in a service industry,' he said. 'Very boring. I'd much rather talk about you.'

'There's not much to talk about.'

'I'm sure there is.'

'I'm afraid I'm a rather dull, suburban housewife who's on her own too much.'

'We can't have that. What suburb?'

'Streatham.'

'What a coincidence. I have a house in Clapham.'

'Just down the road,' said Danielle.

'Isn't it. I must give you my number. If you're ever lonely, I could take you out to dinner sometime. That is if your husband wouldn't object.'

'He'd probably never notice, he's away so much. But

40

I'm sure he wouldn't object even if he did know. He's always telling me I should get out and make more friends.'

'Male friends?'

'Are you asking if he's jealous?'

'Of course. I'd hate to get a punch on the nose because of an innocent dinner.'

'Would it be innocent though?' asked Danielle, recrossing her legs and letting Laurence get a good look at her stocking tops, and a flash of the white skin of her thighs as she did so.

'That would be up to madam.'

'Madam would love to find out,' she said, feeling the brandy warming her body right down to her groin. She crossed her legs again and could feel the wetness in her fanny squelch at the movement. 'And if he is jealous that would be just too bad. It might put some life back into our marriage. And no, he wouldn't punch you on the nose. He's not a violent man. Not over me anyway. But if you interfered with one of his precious sales charts, that might be different.'

Laurence smiled. 'Then it's a date,' he said. 'I'll give you my card,' which he did, and Danielle put it into her bag.

'What are you drinking?' asked Laurence.

'Brandy.'

'Me too. Another coincidence. I hope I'm not being presumptuous, but I have a bottle upstairs in my room, and it's much easier to get served there. Would you like to come up and have a drink? I do have a suite with a sitting room,' he added.

Danielle didn't have to think twice. 'I'd love to,' she said.

They drained their glasses and left the bar together. The barman looked on enviously. I bet he's going to get her knickers off tonight, he thought. Lucky sod.

Danielle and Laurence went upstairs in the lift. When they got to the top floor of the hotel, he led her down the corridor and opened the door to his suite.

The sitting room was about the same size as Danielle's bedroom two floors below. The lights were dim, and the curtains were open to show the view over Southampton to the sea.

'Sit down,' he invited, and she went over to a sofa that looked over the view, and took a seat.

'A brandy wasn't it? he asked, as he walked over to a small bar in the corner.

'This is lovely,' said Danielle. 'You must be very rich.'

'Hardly. I was lucky with some investments a few years back. It seems like ancient history now. But then, with a few thousand pounds, a lot of nerve and even more luck – not to mention some friends in the know . . .' He didn't finish.

'And now you live on the income?'

'Plus the other business I was telling you about. I manage.'

'Very well it seems, by all this.'

'I like to spoil myself when I'm away from home.'

He brought her a large glass, almost half full of amber liquid, and similar for himself. He placed them on the low table in front of the sofa, and sat down next to Danielle.

'You'll get me drunk,' she said as she picked up the glass.

'Cheers,' said Laurence, as he raised his own in a toast.

'To having the best possible time with the best possible people.'

'I'll drink to that,' said Danielle as she touched her glass to his.

'Some music?' asked Laurence.

'Lovely.'

He stood up, went over to a portable CD player that was standing on the sideboard, and touched a button. The room was suddenly full of the muted sound of Stravinsky.

'You must have known I was coming,' said Danielle. 'This is one of my favourites.'

'We aim to please.'

'You do.'

Laurence sat down again, and they listened to the music in silence for a few minutes.

When the piece ended, Laurence got up to change the disc, and Danielle excused herself to use the toilet. Afterwards she stood in his bedroom for a moment before going to the dressing-table to check her make-up again. She sat on the stool and looked at the few articles of male toiletry on top of the table. She sniffed the cap of his cologne bottle and inhaled the masculine freshness of it which she had already smelled on his person.

As she was about to leave the room she noticed something sticking out from under one of the pillows of the double bed. On investigation it turned out to be the shredded remains of a very expensive lilac-coloured silk undergarment. The very same teddy that Laurence had torn from the body of his dinner companion a few hours earlier.

Danielle felt a new rush of excitement as she examined the flimsy article of underwear. She held it up to herself in the mirror of the dressing-table, noting the way the crotch had been ripped out of it, and the way the lace across the bodice had been torn away by strong masculine hands.

She smelt between the legs of it, and thrilled at the musky odour of the unknown woman that lingered on the material. She could almost smell her own musk as her secretions dribbled down to soak the net of her brief panties.

She pulled back the covers of the bed, which she saw had been hastily remade and checked the bottom sheet. On the white material was a pearly-coloured stain that was still wet to the touch. She sniffed her fingers and smelt the feminine musk again, and the male smell of Laurence's juices.

She touched her fingers to her tongue – amazed at her own audacity – put the item of underwear back under the pillow, pulled the bed covers straight again, and returned to the sitting room of the suite.

Laurence had put on a CD by Stevie Wonder and was sitting on the sofa again, gazing out over the lights of the town.

Danielle could hardly contain her sexual excitement. She went and sat next to him so that they were almost touching, picked up her glass and sank half the brandy in one swallow, washing the taste of Laurence and the unknown woman's sex from her lips.

'Everything to your satisfaction?' he asked.

Not until you fuck me rigid, she thought.

'Of course. Wonderful. Are you staying long?' she said.

'I'm off in the morning, back to London.'

'What time are you leaving.'

'Early.'

'Do you want to go to bed?'

'Do you?' he asked, and reached over and touched her hand.

'Soon.'

He leant over further and kissed her on the lips. She opened her mouth and swallowed his tongue, licking at it with her own.

They fell into each other's arms, and Danielle felt his hands roaming her body, and everywhere they touched seemed to burst into flames.

He pushed the skirt of her dress up to her waist, and she climbed into his lap, one thigh on each side of his, pushing herself against his body as their kisses got deeper and more passionate.

She put her hand into his groin and felt his cock rise to do her bidding. He found the zip at the back of her dress and pulled it down. She wriggled out of it and tossed it to the floor, still kissing his face as she did so.

He held her at arm's length, and let his eyes roam over her magnificent body, now clad in only two thin strips of net underwear – which only served to amplify her femininity rather than hide it – suspender belt, and the sheer black stockings that covered her long legs.

'You're beautiful,' he whispered.

'Don't talk,' she said. 'Just love me.'

He pushed her gently off his lap, stood up, and led her to the bedroom.

That was exactly what Danielle wanted. To be fucked in the same bed that Laurence had fucked someone else in earlier. To taste another woman's perfume on his body. To lay her bottom on the wetness that he had made with her, and to plant her wetness on top of it. Like the spoor of the winner in a war of love.

He sat her on the edge of the bed and began to undress. She watched entranced as he took off his jacket, tie, shirt, socks shoes and trousers. His body was tanned and lean and muscular. Finally he stood before her wearing only white boxer shorts through which his erect cock stuck obscenely.

'Pull them down,' he ordered.

She knelt on the carpet in front of him and did as he said. She tugged the shorts over his hips and penis and let them drop to the floor. The sight that presented itself in front of her eyes was the most exciting she'd seen in a day of most exciting sights.

7

The cock that appeared before her eyes was so beautiful it almost took her breath away.

It was long and thick and powerful-looking. It reared from the dark pubic hair that grew thickly at its base, covering the skin of his balls. Like the skin on his prick itself, this too was tan and smooth, with a faint sheen to it, like silk.

'Can I touch it?' she asked.

'Of course.'

She reached out, and felt the weight of it in her palm. It seemed to be sculpted from solid stone, so hard was it – and hot to the touch of her hand.

'It's gorgeous,' she whispered.

'I'm glad you like it.'

'Like it? I love it.'

'Then why don't you?'

She didn't need to be asked twice. She leaned forward and began to lick the wonderful tool. Once again she smelt and tasted the musk of another woman, as well as Laurence's own emissions. It was almost too much for her to bear. She kissed every inch of his gorgeous prick, smearing her lipstick along the length of it, pushing her face into his hair to inhale the stink of love that lingered there.

She kissed her way back to the tip and licked the knob, before opening her lips wide and accepting it into her mouth. His cock filled it, as if made exactly for the task. She licked the underside and then found the little hole at the end with the tip of her tongue and forced it in, until Laurence cried out at the sensation.

She looked up at him and winked, and he winked back. She rode his cock with her mouth, cupping his balls in her hand as she did so, until she knew he was close to climax.

But she wasn't going to give him the satisfaction she'd given Roger earlier, only to be left with the same aching void she'd had when he'd run off back to his wife.

She pulled back from Laurence's penis and said, 'Was that nice?'

'Wonderful. Where did you learn to suck like that?' he asked.

'I'm a natural,' she replied. 'Now fuck me.'

He pulled her to her feet and threw her onto the bed. He didn't take her knickers off, just pushed the gusset to one side and forced her legs roughly open. Then he lay between them and inserted himself inside her pussy. It was easy, so wet and open was it for him.

He was up her in a trice, and she felt the end of his cock riding on her cervix. It was heaven for Danielle. She felt as if she hadn't been fucked for years, so horny was she.

As Laurence rode her, she called for him to go faster, harder. She screamed in his ear, and beat at his back with her fists in passion.

He gladly complied. She smelt so fresh and clean, and her body was young and firm, unlike most of the women he was paid to pleasure by the hour.

He pumped his groin into hers and was rewarded when her breathing became faster, and he knew she was about to come. He drove his cock into her as hard as he could and she laced his back with scratches from her long fingernails.

Normally, Laurence would not countenance treatment like that from women. His body was his living and he liked it in first-class condition. But so engrossed was he with screwing the lithe body that writhed beneath him, that he hardly noticed the pain.

'Yes,' she screamed. 'Yes, you filthy fucker. Give it to me. Give it all to me.'

Harder still he drove himself into her, until the tickling sensation that he began to feel in his scrotum was too much to bear, and with a roar he shot his seed deep into her.

As the milk of his balls burst inside her womb, Danielle pulled Laurence's torso close to her chest and allowed her own orgasm to burst inside her like a flower blooming in the morning sun.

8

Laurence collapsed upon Danielle with a grunt and they both lay as still as death for a few minutes.

Eventually he rolled off her still form and lay on his back on the bed gazing at the ceiling. 'Wonderful,' he said. 'You were bloody wonderful, my darling.'

'Thank you kind sir.' she said, adjusting her knickers to catch the warm juices that were oozing out from between her legs. 'You weren't too bad yourself.'

'Even though I think you've scratched me to the bone. Am I bleeding?'

He rolled over and she examined his back. 'You'll live,' she said.

'I'm glad to hear it. Do you want another drink?'

'Certainly.'

He leaned over and kissed her, then got up, found his robe that was hanging inside the bathroom door, and slipped into it. 'What do you want?' he asked.

'Have you got any mineral water?'

'Of course,' he replied, and left the room.

He returned with another brandy for himself and an iced Perrier for Danielle.

'Are you going to stay the night?' he asked.

'I might. On one condition.'

51

'What's that?'

She turned, crawled up the bed and pulled the lilac-coloured teddy from under the pillow.

'If I can wear this,' she said.

'You little bitch. How did you find that?'

'I saw it when I was in here earlier. You should be more careful when you hide things. Was it fun? Or should I say, was she fun?'

'Not as much fun as you.'

'Was that part of your business earlier.'

'We all have to earn a crust as best we can.'

'A service industry indeed. Servicing women, is that it?'

'As I said. We all have to earn a crust as best we can.'

'You are a filthy bastard.'

'I've been called worse.'

'I bet you have. Tell me about it.'

So he told her.

'My dear Danielle,' he said, 'I was once wealthy. I came from one of the finest families in the land. But unfortunately, being the younger brother I did not inherit a bean. I was forced out into the world to fend for myself as best I could. I discovered I was attractive to women. Especially older women. And, luckily for me, *rich* older women. Or maybe they were the kind I cultivated because of their riches. Early on I decided to make no distinction if they were single, married, divorced or widowed. I cared not if they were beautiful or ugly. Fat or thin. Black or white or yellow. As long as they could supply the one thing I needed. Money.

'I have been escorting women for twenty-five years now. I take them hither and thither and yon. I couldn't care less

52

what we do. Dinner. The theatre. The opera. A day at the races. Whatever they want. And if at the end of the day they invite me to bed, so much the better. All I care about is whether they can afford the price of my company. And I don't come cheaply. Is that too terrible?'

'No,' she said, amazed at what she was saying. But somehow she knew that she had begun to change that day – an irrevocable change for good or bad. But definitely one that would leave her a different person to the one who had left London that morning.

She took the teddy and went to the bathroom, stripped off her bra, knickers, suspender belt and stockings, and put it on. She looked in the mirror and laughed aloud at the sight she presented. She looked, she thought, like a cheap whore. Make-up smeared across her face, her breasts hanging loose through the rips in the lace bodice, and the crotch of the garment hanging down in rags over her come-smeared thighs, leaving the blonde triangle between her legs clearly visible.

She went back to Laurence, who was lounging naked on the bed with a pillow behind his head.

'How *louche*, you look, my darling,' he said. 'Has your husband ever seen you like this?'

'Never.'

'He doesn't know what he's missing.'

'Or what he has,' she said, and she turned and pulled the teddy up around her waist so that he could see the smooth, pink flesh of her buttocks.

His eyes greedily ate up the sight, and the fine tuft of hair that he could see where her legs met at the top.

'Then he's a fool,' he said.

Danielle sat next to Laurence and her hand automatically

went between his legs and she started gently wanking his cock.

His hand moved to her thigh and he rubbed the skin, then slid it up to her cunt and found the messy wetness that he'd been deep inside just a short time before. She scissored her legs wide.

'You want more?' he asked.

'Certainly. You have to leave early and I may never see you again.'

'You will,' he promised, and put his head down into her lap and began licking at the entrance to her cunt.

'Nothing's certain in this world,' she said, biting her lip as the warmth of his mouth seemed to travel right up into the pleasure centres of her brain. She pushed his head deeper into the soft insides of herself.

'In the bed,' she cried. 'Where you had the other woman. I want to feel your wetness on my bottom.'

'You filthy, beautiful whore,' ha said, and stood up and tore the covers off the bed.

Danielle found the wet patch again and lay so that her bottom covered it. At first it was cold, but it soon warmed as her hot flesh heated it up.

Laurence began sucking at her pussy again and as he did she ground herself into the damp sheet beneath her arse.

He rolled her over on to her front and licked at the crack of her buttocks and once again she felt her anus invaded by a man's tongue. She loved the feeling, although it was almost too much to bear – like being tickled too hard.

She rolled back over and found his cock with her mouth and he knelt over her and licked her cunt in perfect time with his cock rubbing between the wet softness of her lips.

Their rhythm increased and she knew that she was going to orgasm again. She didn't know where her sexual energy was coming from, but she loved it.

She sucked harder, and so did Laurence, and as she reached her peak, he shot his warm sticky juice into her mouth. As he came, she pulled his cock out of her mouth and let the semen splash over her face and into her hair.

They lay back together and pulled the covers over themselves.

'I'm so glad we met,' she said.

'Believe me, the feeling is mutual,' he replied.

And that was the last she could remember before she fell asleep.

9

Danielle awoke about eight and for a moment couldn't remember where she was. Or who the handsome man lying next to her was either.

Then the events of the previous day came flooding back and she blushed over her whole body with the remembrance.

My God, she thought, what came over me?

She jumped out of bed, ripped off the remains of the teddy and dropped it to the floor. Then she ran into the bathroom, collected her stained underwear, ran back through the bedroom where Laurence was still asleep and into the sitting room. She shrugged into her dress, stuck her bare feet into her shoes, picked up her handbag and room key and, still running, left the suite and took the stairs down to her own room.

Once inside, she hid her underwear with the stuff she'd worn the previous day, took the phone off the hook, and ran a hot bath.

When she was immersed in the bubble-filled water, she blushed again, but put it down to the heat of the water. She resolved never to do what she had done yesterday, but decided instead to become once more the faithful wife that she had been previously.

But it was such fun, she thought, as she immersed her

whole self under the water and came up blowing like a whale.

She got out of the bath and dived under the shower to wash her hair. Then she dried herself, and got ready to meet her husband.

She reconnected the phone and ordered breakfast in the room. She remembered that Laurence had said he had to leave early, and hoped he'd just go – that he'd get out of her life without trying to speak to her again.

What had happened last night had happened in a vacuum and she didn't need reminding, or to see him ever again.

She needn't have worried, for at that very moment Laurence Stark was steering his S-Type Jaguar out of the parking garage and away in the direction of London.

As he drove, he thought of Danielle.

You may have escaped this morning, my sweet one, he thought, but we'll be together again soon – maybe sooner than either of us could ever imagine. He smiled a saturnine smile and pressed his right foot down on the accelerator of the car.

Danielle had breakfasted by ten-thirty and had dressed in virginal, white silk underwear so fine that she could wear the knickers under trousers. Over the tiny bra and panties she wore white slacks, shirt and shoes. She decided to wait for Nigel in the coffee lounge.

On the way down, she informed the receptionist at the main desk where she was, in case he enquired.

The barman from the previous night was on duty and he smiled as she entered the room.

'Good morning,' he said. 'Did you sleep well?'

'Wonderfully, thank you,' replied Danielle.

'Coffee?' he asked.

'I've just had breakfast. But maybe I could manage a cup.'

'Coming up. Take a seat and I'll bring it over.'

He watched her retreating back and the way her bottom filled the seat of the trousers. No sign of a panty-line, he thought. I wonder if she's wearing any, and he felt his dick stiffen in his trousers at the thought.

He took the coffee over to the table that Danielle had chosen, and asked her if she required a morning paper.

'No, thank you,' she replied.

'Are you staying for the weekend?' asked the barman, pouring her coffee and trying to look down the front of her shirt at the same time.

'For another night,' replied Danielle. 'My husband couldn't make it last night.'

But I bet that other geezer, who was definitely *not* your husband could, thought the barman.

'I hope you can come in and have a drink tonight. I'm in the bar again,' he said.

'Don't you ever take time off?' asked Danielle. 'It sounds like you work all the hours that God sends.'

'Only at the weekend,' replied the young man. 'I take my rest when everyone else is working. The money's better on Fridays and Saturdays. And so are the tips,' he added.

'Then I'd better give you one,' said Danielle.

I wish you would, thought the barman.

Danielle reached into her purse and gave him a pound coin.

'Thank you,' he said.

'And you might get something else later, if you're good,' said Danielle in a throaty voice.

The barman couldn't believe his ears. Was she serious

or was she just teasing him? he wondered.

So did she, but she'd been aware of his attentions the previous evening and this morning, and of the way his eyes kept straying to the hint of cleavage between the buttons of her shirt. She felt like teasing him a little.

'I try to be, always,' he said, and seeing another customer come in, went to serve him.

He had to cover his crotch with the tray on his way back to the bar in case anyone noticed that his cock was almost splitting the material of his trousers.

Nigel arrived just after eleven. He came into the lounge and bounded across the carpet towards Danielle. As he approached, she watched him, comparing him unfavourably with the men she had met the day before.

'Darling,' he cried as he reached her. 'At last. I've missed you terribly.'

'Have you?' asked Danielle.

'Of course. Have you missed me?'

'Terribly,' she replied. 'Now why don't you sit down and join me in a coffee. You can tell me all the exciting news from the conference.'

And that was exactly what Nigel did.

The barman brought more coffee and found another man to envy in Danielle's husband.

Boring, he thought, as he poured Nigel's coffee and heard him pontificating about some minor technical detail of a new multi-transistor. I wonder what he's got that lets her put up with him.

After they'd had coffee, Nigel and Danielle went up to their room. Danielle sat on the bed and thought of what had happened the previous day, as Nigel continued his boring lecture.

As she sat there, she felt herself becoming damp at the thought of the sex she'd experienced. The more she thought about it, the wetter she became, until she could hardly stand the itching between her legs that begged to be scratched by the cock of a horny man.

'Nigel,' she said.

'What darling?'

'Come over here'

'Why?'

'Just come here.'

He did as she asked and she patted the edge of the bed. 'Sit down,' she said.

He did as she asked again and she said, 'Nigel, darling, I did miss you last night.'

'Did you?'

She ran her hand down his arm and replied, 'Yes. Most awfully.'

'I am so sorry, darling,' he said. 'You know I would have been here if I could.'

'I know. But now you're here, couldn't we . . .?'

'What?'

'You know.'

'I thought we were going out for lunch.'

'We could make it a late lunch.'

'But I thought we could take a drive out and find a nice pub.'

'Nigel, I'd rather stay here with you.'

'We've got all day, darling.'

I haven't, she thought, if I don't get hold of a hard cock soon, I'll die.

She leant over and kissed him. Then the phone rang.

'Christ!' she said, as he picked it up.

61

'Terrance,' he said. 'How did you know I was here?'

There was a pause.

'Oh, Charles told you. What can I do for you?'

There was a longer pause.

'I see,' said Nigel. 'Hold on one second.'

'Darling,' he said to Danielle, covering the mouthpiece of the phone with his hand. 'It's Terrance Stride. VIP customer. He needs a few minutes of my time. Could I meet you downstairs in the lounge. I won't be long. Promise.'

Danielle got to her feet. 'Yes,' she said. 'Anything you say. Business before pleasure as always.' And she walked out of the room, slamming the door behind her hard.

Nigel looked at the door in puzzlement. What is the matter with the girl today, he thought. And went back to his call.

10

At the door of the coffee lounge, she met the young barman coming out.

'Hello,' he said. 'Are you after more coffee?'

'Yes. My husband has to take a very important business call, so the little woman has to make herself scarce.'

'I'm afraid my colleague will have to look after you, I'm on my break.'

Danielle looked at his strong chest in the tight waistcoat he wore and, still aware of the wetness in the crotch of her silken knickers, and of the itching that seemed to fill her cunt to overflowing, said, 'Can we go somewhere?'

'Sorry?' said the barman.

'Somewhere private where we can be alone for a few minutes.'

'I'm sorry, I don't underst . . .'

'I want to fuck you,' said Danielle. 'And I know you want to fuck me. Don't you?'

The young man was thunderstruck. He couldn't believe he was hearing correctly.

'I . . . I . . . I' he stammered.

'You do, don't you?' she asked. 'I've been watching the way you look at me.'

He nodded. Speechless.

'It's all right,' said Danielle. 'No one will know. Just tell me where, and I'll meet you.'

The boy's mind raced.

'There's a cleaning cupboard,' he said. 'Just round the corner of the corridor.' He pointed in front of him. 'Third door on the left.' Then he cursed himself for his stupidity. A woman like this, he thought. In a cleaning cupboard. Boy, have I blown it.

Danielle smiled wickedly. 'Perfect,' she said. 'An adventure. I love adventures.'

He walked off in the direction he'd indicated and after a few seconds Danielle followed. The cupboard door was ajar and she pushed it open and slid inside.

He was standing in the midst of brooms, brushes, mops, Hoovers, buckets and all sorts of cleaning materials. The cupboard smelt of bleach and Danielle had to stifle a laugh. Really, Mrs Morgan, she thought. Has your whole life led to this?

She pushed the door closed behind her. Her fingers found the light switch and a dim bulb in the ceiling clicked on.

Even in its faint light she saw that he was aroused.

Without any foreplay she undid the zip on her pants and shoved them down, followed by the white silk panties she was wearing.

'Come on then,' she said. 'You want it don't you?'

He tried to kiss her, but she moved her head away. 'Mind my make-up,' she said. 'Do you want it or not?'

He did. He unzipped himself, and dropped his trousers and underpants too.

Danielle was aware of the comical sight they must have made, but she didn't care.

He was the perfect height to stick his dick straight into her pussy, so she pulled him close, and climbed aboard the hot meat of it.

It slid straight up her wet love-canal and he started humping her, which was just what she wanted. She kept her head turned away as he worked his knob up and down the length of her cunt until, with a hoarse cry, he came.

Danielle squeezed her legs together on his prick, but he'd come too early and her orgasm was still miles away. But at least she'd been penetrated and the immediate itch of desire was sated.

'Short and sweet,' she said, as she slid off him and pulled up her pants and trousers. 'That's how I like it.'

Then she pecked his cheek, opened the door of the cupboard, peered down the corridor to make sure the coast was clear, and left without as much as a backward glance.

Bitch, she thought as she went back to the coffee lounge. But at least it was better than nothing.

Better than Nigel, anyway.

But what wasn't?

11

Nigel arrived before the barman returned from his break.

Just as well, thought Danielle. That would have made an interesting tableau.

'Everything's fine,' said Nigel. 'Terrance is well and truly satisfied.'

I wish I was, thought Danielle.

'And now let's go,' said her husband. 'Before someone else catches me.'

'What about your car phone?' asked Danielle drily.

'I'll disconnect it. And talking of car phones I spoke to young Roger on the way up this morning. He was singing your praises as a hostess to the skies.'

'Is that right?' asked Danielle.

'Absolutely. Couldn't have been more effusive. He's invited us to stay the next time we're in the area.'

I just bet he has, thought Danielle. All the better to get me in some corner, sucking him off again. Dream on, sonny.

'That would be nice. I'd love to meet his wife,' she said.

'And so you shall. Lunch? Roger recommended a place. A pub miles from anywhere that has the most amazing restaurant apparently.'

They left the hotel, and Nigel fetched his black BMW 5-series saloon from the garage. When she got in, Danielle was pleased to see the car phone had been turned off.

They drove out of town into the country, and at twelve-thirty Nigel parked the car in front of a large country pub lying at the foot of a wooded hill.

'Excellent,' he said as he climbed out. 'I hope the food is as good as the view.'

They went inside and had an excellent lunch. Afterwards, Nigel asked Danielle what she'd like to do for the rest of the afternoon.

Get fucked, she thought. I want to come so badly I can't stand it.

'Let's go for a drive,' she said. 'Get a bottle of wine from behind the bar and find somewhere quiet to stop and drink it.'

'A great idea,' agreed Nigel, and called for the bill. When it came he asked for a bottle of chilled white wine to be added to it, and negotiated the cost of two glasses and a corkscrew.

He settled up with his credit card, and he and Danielle left the pub and drove further into the countryside. Eventually Danielle pointed to a leafy lane off the main road, and said, 'Let's try up there.'

Nigel pulled the car into the lane, and drove slowly up it, until they came to a clearing surrounded by trees. A stream gurgled between the thick grass that covered the floor of the clearing.

'This is perfect,' said Danielle, 'Let's stop and have a drink.'

Nigel brought the car to a halt, and switched off the engine. It was perfectly quiet inside the forest. They got out of the car and Nigel opened the bottle and filled the two glasses.

'You are clever, Nigel,' said Danielle. 'Remembering the corkscrew and all. I would never have thought of that.'

Screw, she mused. Now that's a good word.

They sat together on the warm grass and raised their glasses to toast each other.

'Here's to us,' said Nigel. 'Together forever.'

Danielle smiled, and lay back on the grass, opening her legs slightly as she did so.

'Darling,' she said, 'Let's make love.'

'Here? In the open?' said Nigel. 'What if someone comes?'

Who cares, thought Danielle. Let them come. As long as I do.

'No one will, darling,' she said. 'I bet no one but us has been up here for years.'

'I don't know,' said Nigel. 'I suppose it would be all right.'

Danielle pulled him down beside her. 'Kiss me,' she demanded.

Nigel leaned down and pecked at her lips.

'No. Kiss me. Like you mean it. Like a man who knows his woman needs to be loved.'

He kissed her harder, but still she wasn't satisfied with his ministrations.

'Harder,' she begged. 'Hurt me Nigel.'

Nigel had never heard his wife talk like this before. 'Are you all right?' he asked. 'Are you sure you didn't have something suspect at lunch?'

God, she thought, what a prat.

She grabbed him and dragged him down beside her,

spilling his wine in the process.

'Careful,' he said.

'I don't feel like being careful. I feel like being fucked,' she retorted.

'Very well,' he said. 'Then you shall.'

At last, she thought.

Nigel began to caress her and she kissed him with fresh abandon. He stroked her body from breast to thigh and she felt that warm horny feeling wash over her again in waves of pleasure.

She kissed him hard on the mouth and at last he began to respond. Their mouths opened and their tongues played together.

Danielle pushed herself hard against her husband's body, and she felt his cock stirring in response.

She smiled to herself, and put her hand down between his legs.

'Undress me,' she said.

He quickly unbuttoned her blouse and slid it off her shoulders. She kicked off her shoes, and he undid her trousers and pulled them down. Her bra was next to go, revealing the beauty of her breasts, and her nipples – red and engorged with blood – stood out, ready to be sucked. Nigel put his mouth on first one then the other. The sensation went down to Danielle's pussy which was still full of the barman's come from their close encounter earlier that morning.

Danielle tore at Nigel's clothes as he licked and sucked at the teats of her breasts. She stripped him to the waist, then undid the zip on his trousers.

She tugged them and his underpants down together and his prick was revealed.

Not too bad, she thought. Not quite up to some of the giants she'd seen recently, but very acceptable nevertheless.

She took it in her hand and gently massaged the tip with her thumb.

'God, darling, that's beautiful,' Nigel said.

'Take off my knickers,' ordered Danielle, and within a second her flimsy silk briefs joined the rest of her clothes on the grass and she was naked in front of her husband.

Nigel pulled the rest of his clothes off and said, 'Come here, I want to fuck you.'

'You'll have to catch me first,' said Danielle, who now that she was sure of being screwed, wanted to prolong the pleasure of anticipation, and she ran across the grass-covered floor of the clearing.

Nigel chased after her. She dodged round one of the tree trunks, and he grabbed her arm and threw her to the ground.

She lay with arms and legs open. 'Lick me first,' she said wickedly. Exactly how wickedly Nigel didn't realise: or that her cunt was still full of another man's cream. The remnants of a hasty fuck, earlier in the day.

He fell between her legs and stuck his tongue into the entrance of her pussy. It tasted musky and sour, but in his present state of arousal, he hardly noticed. If anything, he thought that he had never tasted anything as delicious.

His tongue worked around the wet delicacy inside his wife's cunt. Then he pushed deeper and soon his face was covered in slimy mucus. He moved up Danielle's body and began to kiss her mouth. She thrilled as she licked at the love-juice on his face. The fact that he was ignorant of what it was excited her even more.

I wonder what he'd say if I told him, she thought. For a moment she was tempted, but managed to resist.

She could feel his prick pushing at the entrance to the delights of her cunt, and she put her hand down and found her slit with the tip of Nigel's cock and allowed it free entry.

One again she felt the thrill as his meat slid up into the centre of her very being.

God, she thought, after all this time, I've at last discovered the joy of being screwed. Better late than never.

He moved inside her and her cunt muscles tensed and relaxed as he slowly at first, then faster, manipulated his prick inside her.

'That's lovely,' she panted. 'I love it when you do that.'

He moved even faster inside her and she felt him tense as he was about to come.

'No, she cried. 'Not yet.' He stopped on the brink of orgasm, and she felt his whole body trembling with the effort of holding his jism inside himself. Like a rocket being fired into orbit, she felt her own orgasm begin way at the top of her womb and burst outwards until it engulfed her whole body, and she screamed, 'Now!' and he plunged himself into her one last time, before shooting his load as deeply inside her as he had ever reached before.

12

When Danielle and Nigel got back to the hotel, they showered and changed, and went down for dinner. They were both ravenous after their open air love-making, and demolished a fillet mignon between them, followed by the 'Lover's Special' dessert – a dish of a dozen different flavoured ice creams served up for two.

'What do you fancy doing this evening, darling?' asked Nigel, once their coffee and liqueurs had been served and the waiter had disappeared.

'I don't know,' replied Danielle. 'How about you?'

'A drink in the bar maybe, followed by an early night.'

'Sounds delicious,' his wife replied. She had enjoyed her sex with him that afternoon immensely and wouldn't mind a second helping at all.

They went into the bar together and Danielle smiled at the young barman – her conquest from that morning – who blushed slightly, and smiled back.

Nigel led her to a seat in the corner and went to the bar to order the brandy she had requested, and one for himself.

As he was standing there, the door of the bar opened and Roger Clinton entered with a tall, pretty, dark-haired woman wearing a blue dress.

'Nigel,' said Roger. 'I thought you might be here still. I

had a call from Terrance Stride. He said that you'd spoken this morning, and that you were staying an extra night.'

'Was the old boy happy?' asked Nigel.

'Ecstatic. There's a big order on the way, or I'm a Dutchman. Sorry,' he said to his wife, who had pulled a cross face. 'Mustn't talk shop. Nigel, you remember my wife, Anne?'

'How could I forget?' asked Nigel gallantly. 'I hear you had problems last night and couldn't make it.'

'The baby-sitter,' she replied in a soft voice. 'I *was* disappointed that I missed my dinner.'

'I made up for it tonight though,' said Roger. 'A slap-up meal at the new Thai restaurant in town. Then I thought we'd pop in to see if you were around. I had to dash off last night and I wanted to apologise to your wife.'

'No apology necessary, I'm sure,' said Nigel. 'But what a kind thought. She's sitting over in the corner. Can I get you two a drink?'

'Marvellous,' said Roger. 'This time the baby-sitter's booked until one. I'll have a beer. And you Anne?'

'A Grand Marnier,' she replied. 'That'll finish off the evening wonderfully.'

'Not quite the finish, I hope,' said Nigel. 'You must join us until you have to get home. This *is* a marvellous surprise.'

Not quite so marvellous for Danielle. She greeted the new arrivals warmly enough, but she had far from forgiven Roger for deserting her in her hour of sexual need the previous evening.

They sat together and Nigel said. 'I believe there's dancing in the ballroom on a Saturday evening. I saw the notice on my way in. Is anyone interested?'

'I love dancing,' said Anne Clinton. 'And it's been an age. Shall we Roger?'

'Certainly. If Mrs Morgan would like to,' Roger replied.

'Call me Danielle, please.' You little twerp, she thought. Coming creeping round here with your dull wife in tow. I think it's about time I taught you a lesson.

'And of course I'd love to go dancing. It'll round off our day perfectly,' she added.

'Then dancing it is,' said Nigel.

They left the bar and went into the ballroom where a small band had set up in one corner and were playing a selection of Broadway musical standards. In the opposite corner was a bar. Nigel made straight for it and ordered another round of drinks.

They all took seats at a table at the side of the dance floor and, as the band segued from 'On The Street Where You Live' to 'I'm Gonna Wash That Man Right Out Of My Hair', Roger said to Danielle, 'Would you care to dance?'

'I'd be delighted,' she replied, and they both stood up and walked together to the floor.

'You look lovely tonight,' said Roger, as he took Danielle into his arms and propelled her out into the throng of dancers.

'I thought I was just a distraction. At least that's what you told your wife last night when she phoned up and ordered you home.'

'I'm so sorry,' he said. 'We've been having problems at home for months. I just couldn't face another row.'

'I don't know,' said Danielle. 'I don't know if I can forgive you.'

'Please do. I came here especially to see you tonight

and explain. And I'm glad I did. I meant what I said about you looking beautiful. You do.'

Danielle – dressed in a short red evening gown, red shoes, dark stockings, and red silk underwear – ate up the compliment. She was glad now that she'd brought a spare dress with her, because the black one she'd worn the evening before was creased from lying on Laurence's floor all night.

'Do you think so?'

'I do. Nigel is such a lucky man. Having someone like you.'

'You don't know what someone like me is like.'

'I can imagine.'

Don't stretch your imagination too far, Buster Brown, she thought, you might stretch a muscle in your brain.

Roger pulled her closer as the music got slower and she could feel the shape of his erection teasing her between her legs.

She wanted to ask if it was a pistol or was he just glad to see her? but resisted. He probably wouldn't get the joke, she thought.

Instead she said, 'That feels nice.'

'Yes it does,' he replied, and pushed himself even closer.

'Don't let Nigel see,' she said. 'Or Anne.'

'I don't think Anne would care much,' replied Roger.

'Nigel would,' said Danielle, and Roger eased the pressure on her groin.

'You don't have to stop altogether. I quite like it.'

'Only quite?' he asked.

'I'll tell you later,' she said, and squeezed his arm.

'I'll look forward to that.'

'What about Anne?'

'I'll worry about her,' he said.

I bet you will, thought Danielle.

After two dances they returned to the table.

'Our turn,' said Nigel, holding out his hand to Anne Clinton, and they left Roger and Danielle to take to the dance floor themselves.

'Another drink?' asked Roger.

'Yes please.'

He called over the waiter and ordered another round. Then he slid his foot up Danielle's nylon-clad calf and said, 'They seem to be getting on very well,' looking in the direction of Anne and Nigel.

'Matchmaking?' asked Danielle.

'Would you mind?'

'If Nigel and your wife ended up in bed? Not really. As long as they had a good time. Do you think they would?'

'I don't know. It's been so long since I've made love to my wife, I can hardly remember what it's like.'

'You have a baby.'

'A two-year-old bouncing boy. And I don't think I've slept with her in *that* way more than once or twice since he was born.'

Liar, thought Danielle.

'Poor you,' she sympathised.

'That was why I was so disappointed when I had to rush off last night.'

'I'm sure you were.'

'It could have been very good.'

'Wasn't what I did to you very good, then?'

'Of course. It was wonderful, but I wanted to do something for you in return.'

I just bet you did, thought Danielle.

'And I wanted you to,' she said.

'I was devastated I had to leave you unsatisfied.'

Don't worry, thought Danielle. I was more than well taken care of later.

'Devastated,' she said. 'So was I.'

'Do you think we could . . .?'

'What?'

'You know.'

'Are you serious?'

'Of course. I could make up for last night, right now.'

'What now? Here? With our partners with us?'

'Wouldn't that excite you?' he asked.

As a matter of fact it did excite her. Tremendously.

She smiled. 'Yes. It would, Roger. In fact I can feel it exciting me already.'

She'd experienced a sudden warm rush between her legs, and her knees felt as if they wouldn't support her if she stood up.

He smiled. 'Shall we, then?'

'Yes let's,' said Danielle. 'Let's be naughty. I'd like that very much.'

'Where?' asked Roger.

Danielle looked over at the dance floor. Nigel and Anne had just started another dance together. She looked at the door, and wondered how they could make their escape long enough for her to get Roger's dick inside her.

'Where's your car?' she asked.

'In the garage.'

'What level?'

'The first.'

'When they get back, tell them you've got to get something from it.'

'What?'

'Christ, I don't know. Anything. Use a little imagination, Roger.'

I hope you've got more nous when you're screwing, she thought. Or this is going to be a waste of time.

'Then I'll tell them I've got a bit of a headache and want to get a pill from our room.'

'What room are you in?'

'No,' she said. 'Not the room. I'll meet you at your car.'

Roger grinned. 'That sounds fine,' he said.

'What make is it?'

'A BMW 3-Series. Dark red. It's parked in the corner furthest from the lift.'

'I'll find it.'

Roger winked and said, 'They're coming back.'

Nigel and Anne sat back down and Roger said, 'Nigel. You remember that report I owe you?'

Nigel nodded.

'I think I put it in the car. I'll go and get it.'

'There's no rush,' said Nigel. 'It is Saturday night.'

'No problem,' said Roger. 'I won't be a mo. Excuse me all.' He got up and, with a smile to everyone at the table, left the ballroom.

'How are you darling?' asked Nigel.

'I've got a bit of a head actually,' said Danielle, glad that her husband had raised the subject. 'I think I'll go and get a pill from the room.'

'I'll go,' said Nigel.

'You don't know where they are, darling,' she said with a look at Anne that said 'Men'.

Anne smiled back.

'Maybe they've got something behind the bar,' said Nigel.

'You know I can only take my special headache pills,' said Danielle. 'Everything else disagrees with me. I won't be long. Have another dance. Enjoy yourselves.'

I intend to. She thought.

'Do you want me to come with you?' asked Anne.

Crikey, thought Danielle, getting away from these two is like getting out of Colditz.

'No,' she said. 'Stay and keep Nigel company.' With that she got up, and she too left the ballroom.

As soon as she was outside, she sped down a corridor in the direction of the 'EXIT-CAR PARK' sign.

She caught the empty lift down to the first level, and walked through the ranks of parked cars in the direction that Roger had told her, until she spotted him standing beside a maroon BMW.

As she arrived beside him, he opened the back door. 'Hop in,' he said.

She did as he bade and slid along the leather upholstered seat. He joined her, closing the door behind himself.

As soon as the courtesy light went out, he grabbed her and pulled her close to kiss him.

Slow down, boy, she thought, but returned his kisses enthusiastically after a moment.

His hands were all over her body and she felt a new rush of excitement between her legs.

She groped for his prick and felt the hardness of it through the soft material of his trousers. She scrambled to undo them as he pushed her skirt up to her waist, and ripped at the flimsy knickers that were all between him and the delicious heat of her snatch.

She felt the material part as he tore them from her body, and she tugged his trousers down to his knees, lying back on the cool leather of the seat, opening her legs wide.

She could smell her own musk in the confines of the car as Roger knelt between her legs. She moved her bottom to the edge of the seat, and shoved his meat up into the softness of her aching pussy.

As his prick filled her to bursting point, she came onto it. A long boiling come that transported her to paradise.

'There,' he said. 'Was it worth the wait?'

'Yes,' she cried. 'Now fuck me hard, I want another.'

He did exactly as she ordered him.

He moved in and out of her and the car rocked with the violence of his assault on her quim.

Quicker and quicker he fucked at her soft body, until she could bear it no longer and she came again, hugging his body close to hers, and rubbing herself off against him in an ecstasy of sexual excitement.

'I'm going to come,' he cried. 'I want you. I need you.' And with a fresh burst of pumping, he shot his jism into her core, and collapsed across her body.

13

They lay together for a moment, shuddering in the aftermath of their orgasms, before Danielle tapped Roger on the shoulder and said, 'Don't you think we'd better be getting back before someone sends out a search party for us?'

'Oh Christ,' he said, pushing himself off her so that his shrinking cock popped out of her with an audible plop. 'You're right. I forgot all about *them*.'

That was exactly what Danielle wanted to hear.

'And so you should have,' she said. 'You had much more important things to concentrate on.'

Roger kissed her and said, 'Look, I'll get back. I'll flannel Nigel that I left the report on my desk at home. You wait a few minutes, OK?'

'Certainly. I'll have to do my make-up. You've smeared it everywhere.'

'Was it worth it?' Roger asked.

'Of course, darling. Now do hurry, and leave the door, so that the little light stays on.'

Roger struggled to pull up his trousers, fastened them, and tucked in his shirt. He got out of the car and made off in the direction of the lift.

Danielle straightened her skirt and took her make-up

bag from her handbag. By the time she had found a tissue to clean off the worst of the mess Roger had made of her mascara, she'd forgotten all about him.

When she was satisfied she could pass muster back in the light, she too left the car. Before she went, she bunched up the red silk knickers that Roger had torn off her hips and stuffed them between the cushions of the back seat. She smiled as she stood up, and felt the mixture of her's and Roger's wetness trickle out of her slit, down her thighs to the top of her stockings.

When she got back to the ballroom, Nigel was only interested in her state of health, but she saw Anne Clinton examining her clothes closely with her eyes and guessed that she was suspicious about the fact that Danielle and her husband had been absent at the same time.

From previous experience, I expect, thought Danielle. You don't have to worry darling, I wouldn't have him if he came with Green Shield stamps.

Nigel ordered another round of drinks, then begged Danielle to dance with him. She was going to refuse, pleading the excuse of her fictitious headache, but accepted after a moment. She wanted to leave Anne and Roger together for a few minutes. She had the feeling that once they were alone, sparks might fly.

And looking over from where she and Nigel were dancing together, it looked as if she was right.

Anne was going head to head with Roger at the table and he looked as if he'd rather be anywhere except where he was sitting.

Serves you right, you sneaky little bastard, thought Danielle.

When the tune had finished, she and Nigel went back to

the table and Roger said, 'I think it's about time we were going, Nigel.'

'So soon?' said Nigel. 'I thought you had ages yet.'

'Well, you know how it is. Got to watch the drinking and driving. They're very hot on that in this area. And I don't want to lose my licence.'

'Quite right,' said Nigel. 'I admire your self-control. Tonight I'm the lucky one who won't be driving.'

Anne sat glowering at Danielle, who smiled sweetly back at her and said, 'We really must do this again, the next time we're in the area.'

'Yes, of course,' said Anne in reply, but she sounded as if she were about to choke.

'That's a date then,' said Nigel. 'I'll be looking forward to it.'

Roger and Anne made their final farewells and left the ballroom.

'What a marvellous couple,' said Nigel. 'I do like them. They're such good company.'

'Aren't they?' said Danielle. 'I can't wait to see them again.'

'I'm so pleased,' said Nigel. 'It always makes life easier when you get on with the staff and their families. I was a bit worried dumping him on you last night.'

'I get on very well with Roger,' said Danielle. 'Whatever made you think I wouldn't?'

14

The next morning Danielle and Nigel drove their separate
cars back to their detached house in one of the more
picturesque parts of the south London suburb of Streatham.
After a few days back in her old routine, Danielle almost
came to believe that she had dreamed her adventures during
her visit to Southampton.

But sometimes, whilst she was out shopping, or doing
the housework or cooking Nigel's evening meal, she'd
suddenly remember, and blush with a mixture of excitement
and shame at the memories.

On the Thursday after they returned, at about two in the
afternoon, Danielle had just finished watching 'Neighbours',
when the front door bell rang.

She frowned and switched off the TV set. She wasn't
expecting visitors or any deliveries and, with a puzzled
look on her face, she went to answer the door.

Laurence Start was standing on the doorstep holding an
enormous bunch of red roses.

'*Laurence*,' said Danielle in amazement. 'What are you
doing here? How did you know that I lived here?'

'Darling,' replied Laurence. 'After you fled without a
word the other morning, I invested twenty pounds in one
of the receptionists at the hotel and he kindly gave me the

87

address of the charming lady I'd chatted with the previous evening, so that I could send her a letter of thanks. I hope you're not cross with me.'

Danielle didn't know *what* she was. One part of her was furious that Laurence had come to the house. Another part was pleased. Another part was filled with such a rush of sexual excitement that she could hardly stand still. And yet another part was scared stiff that a neighbour would see him, and tell Nigel.

'Are you just going to leave me standing on the doorstep?' asked Laurence.

'Yes . . . No . . . I don't know. You shouldn't have come. What would my husband say?'

'I thought you said he wouldn't even notice.'

'He might not, but there are a few old biddies around here who will. They're probably peering through the curtains now. And they'll only be too pleased to let him know all about it.'

'Invite me in then. These roses will wilt if they don't get into water soon.'

Danielle hesitated, then opened the door wide to allow him entry. He stepped into the hall and she closed the door firmly behind him, to keep prying eyes out.

'Go into the living room,' she said, and showed him to the first door on the left down the hall. As she did so, she noticed her reflection in the mirror by the coat rack. She was still wearing the track suit which she'd put on that morning to do the shopping and housework.

I look a fright, she thought.

'Give me those,' she said, taking the roses from Laurence. 'I'll put them into water. Help yourself to a drink, I won't be a moment.'

She sped into the kitchen, found a vase, filled it with water and stood the roses untidily in it. Then she went back into the hall and upstairs to make herself look more presentable.

She stripped down to her underwear – a basic white cotton bra from Marks and Sparks, with matching briefs – and rummaged in her wardrobe until she found a plain black skirt and a white blouse. She looked at her reflection, and once again felt the mixture of fury, pleasure, sexual excitement and fear that she'd experienced when she'd seen Laurence at the door.

She combed her hair and put on some make-up, then hesitated before getting dressed.

To hell with it, she thought. It won't hurt if I change my undies for something a little more exotic. *He* doesn't have to know. Though with another thrill of excitement she thought that he just might.

She undid her bra and threw it into the wash basket, peeled off the panties, and went to her underwear drawer. She chose a tiny, white bra with a matching G-string which was really just a triangle of lace with a strip of elastic round the waist, and a narrow piece of material that went between her legs and the crack of her buttocks, leaving the twin orbs of her bottom totally uncovered. Where the G-string fitted over her cunt, the thin cloth slid into the wetness there, and as she moved it pushed up into the delicate membrane and irritated her clitoris in a most pleasant way.

She pulled on the undies, then hastily donned the short skirt and blouse, pushed her bare feet into ridiculously high-heeled black shoes and checked herself once more in the mirror. Once satisfied, she went downstairs to her surprise guest.

Laurence was sitting on the sofa in the living-room with a glass of amber liquid in his hand.

'You've changed,' he said. 'You look lovely. I thought you were the char at first.'

'Very funny,' said Danielle. 'Now exactly what are you doing here uninvited?'

'I wondered why you left without saying goodbye the other morning.'

'My husband was on his way. You know that.'

'Even so. Didn't you enjoy our night together?'

'I was drunk.'

'So was I. But that didn't stop me enjoying it.'

'I don't usually do things like that.'

'Nevertheless you did.'

Danielle thought back to their night together and her stomach slipped at the thought of being in the circle of his strong arms. She remembered the way his cock had pushed up inside her, how the hot jet of his semen had bubbled up into her womb, and she felt herself weakening at the memory.

'Maybe I did, So what?'

'Don't worry. I'm not going to tell anyone. I just thought we might renew our friendship. You did say I could take you out to dinner one night.'

'I did, didn't I?' said Danielle, and she smiled.

'Is it still on?' asked Laurence.

'I don't see why not. But you shouldn't have come here.'

'No one will know.'

'I wouldn't be so sure of that.'

'I was very discreet, I parked my car round the corner.'

'Discreet? Do you call it discreet to turn up on my

doorstep with a dozen red roses.'

'You can tell anyone who's interested that it was a delivery from Interflora.'

Danielle smiled. 'So I could,' she said. 'Did you pour a drink for me?'

'I thought I'd leave that up to you.'

Danielle went to the drinks cupboard and helped herself to a large scotch. Then she went to the armchair opposite him and sat down, allowing the skirt she was wearing to slide up the smooth skin of her bare thighs.

'Cheers,' she said.

'Cheers,' he replied. 'How have you been?'

'Bored,' she said. 'Just like a suburban housewife should be.'

Laurence smiled and she saw his eyes shift down to look at her long legs.

She wriggled as the material of the G-string bit into the softness between them again, and her skirt slid still further up her thighs.

'So where's your husband today?' asked Laurence.

'At a sales meeting.'

'Where?'

'Bedfordshire.'

'When will he be back?'

She smiled. She knew exactly what Laurence had come for and she debated whether or not to give it to him.

'Late.'

'How late?'

Late enough, she thought.

'Ten, eleven.'

Laurence smiled too. 'Perhaps we could have dinner tonight.'

'Perhaps we could.'

He drained his glass. 'May I have another?' he asked.

'Of course,' replied Danielle.

'And for you?'

She finished her drink with a gulp and felt the warmth of the liquor make its way down to her stomach. 'Please,' she said.

Laurence collected her glass and went and poured fresh scotch into both.

'You have a very nice house,' he said when he was seated again.

'Not bad.'

'I'd say a lot better than that.'

'Would you like to look round?' asked Danielle.

She knew that he was looking for any excuse to get her into the bedroom and, after drinking scotch on an empty stomach, she didn't mind one bit.

'I'd love to.'

They both stood and Danielle took him on a short tour of the ground floor and then upstairs.

'This is the master bedroom,' she said as they entered hers and Nigel's bedroom.

'It's lovely,' said Laurence, then he noticed her discarded knickers on the carpet. 'I hope you've got some on,' he said. 'Or else you'll catch your death.'

'That's for me to know and you find out,' said Danielle coquettishly, and before she knew it she was in his arms and they were kissing passionately.

Laurence held her close, and she could feel the shape of his cock as it hardened between his legs. She pulled him towards the bed, and they tumbled across it together.

Laurence tugged off his jacket, and she tore the buttons

from his shirt, so impatient was she to feel the bare skin of his chest against her.

Likewise, he ripped at her blouse, and the buttons skittered across the carpet as the material parted.

He pushed her bra straps off her shoulders, and tugged the brief laciness of the garment down from her breasts without unfastening the snaps at the back. Then he was on her tits with his mouth, like a starving baby.

He bit at the tenderness of the engorged nipples until she cried out with pleasure so intense it was like pain.

She fumbled blindly with the fastenings of his trousers and when she felt them open, she pushed them down his legs.

Laurence pulled at the zip of her skirt and stripped it down over her hips and buttocks. She locked her mouth to his wetly and pulled him on top of her. She felt his naked prick rock hard and hot against her thigh and felt herself, still moist from before, responding once more, flooding with fresh wetness as his fingers found the wisp of material that was all that covered her pussy.

He pushed the strip of material to one side and entered her with deliberate abruptness, thrust once, quickly and deep, then almost withdrew, lying just inside her with a stillness that excited her until she found herself bucking eagerly beneath him, words babbling from her lips. The filthiest words she could imagine. A stream of obscenities that made him forget everything and start to pump in a deep rhythm of satisfying thrusts. She met them eagerly, arching her body as his head went down, and his mouth fed on her nipples again. They were lost to everything but their coupling. In a deep, silent exchange of pleasure, with no sound but the slap of their flesh or a quiet moan. As the fuck went on, Danielle wrapped her long legs around Laurence, straining her sex to be even closer to his. To have his prick even deeper inside her. They built and built until finally, helplessly, the wave in them broke and together they convulsed, Laurence's long roar of pleasure drowning Danielle's cries.

Then they lay, still locked together, exhausted and satisfied.

'Are you glad I came?' asked Laurence.

'In more ways than you'll ever know,' Danielle whispered back.

15

Laurence lay perfectly still on top of Danielle and she loved the feeling of his weight on her body.

After a few minutes he rolled off her with a moan and as his prick slid out of her cunt she felt empty inside all of a sudden. She found his cock with her hand, and began to stroke the wetness of the skin.

'More?' he asked. 'So soon. You are a randy little cow, aren't you?'

'Yes,' she said. 'I hate it when you desert me.'

'You deserted me last week.'

'That was different. I couldn't have my husband come back and find me in another man's room. Let alone his bed, with his come dribbling out of me.'

'Do you think he'd be angry with you?'

'I certainly hope so. Wouldn't you be?'

'It depends. If I loved you. I'd want you to experience as much pleasure as possible. If I wasn't there, and you took it with another man, how could I be angry?'

'You're just a pervert, Laurence,' she said. But his words excited her in a strange way and her pussy oozed juice again.

Christ, she thought. I'm sure I'm turning into a nymphomaniac.

As her hand gently kneaded the flesh of his penis, she began to feel it respond again and the ooze turned to a flood.

'I need a cigarette first,' said Laurence. 'You're quite an exhausting woman. Fetch me one from my jacket and go and get me another drink.'

'I want to be fucked again first,' complained Danielle.

Laurence's hand connected with her buttock with a crack and she jumped at the pain of the blow.

'Don't argue,' he said. 'Do as I say, bitch, or there'll be more of that.'

Danielle thrilled at the blow and loved the way he ordered her around as if she were a slave. She wished that Nigel would treat her that way, instead of trying to pander to her every whim.

She jumped off the bed and, ignoring the jism that leaked from her cunt and ran stickily down her leg, she picked up Laurence's jacket. She found his cigarettes and lighter, extracted a cigarette from the packet and gave it to him. Then she lit it.

'Ashtray.'

'Downstairs,' she said.

'Get it then, and that drink.'

She ran downstairs, naked, and sloshed whisky into their glasses, grabbed an ashtray from the coffee table and went back up to where Laurence was waiting, lying naked on the bed with his cock half erect, smoking his cigarette.

She caught the length of ash off it with the ashtray and gave him his drink.

'Suck me, whilst I finish this,' he said. 'Then I'll fuck you again.'

Without a word she went down on the dampness of his

cock. She loved the taste of her juice and his come that was mixed on his skin. She sucked at him eagerly and soon she felt his meat grow hard in her mouth.

She sucked and licked at it until it was rigid again. When he stubbed out his cigarette, she mounted him and slid his cock up between the lips of her pussy, riding him like a jockey.

She bore down on his balls and felt the knob of his cock hard up inside her, exciting her cervix until she could hardly bear the sensation. She came again with a squeal, looking down on him as he calmly looked up at her, as if they were doing nothing more exciting than discussing the weather.

Bastard, she thought. You may be cool now, but by the time I've finished with you, you'll be begging for it. You wait and see.

'Good?' he asked.

'Not bad,' she said.

'Is that all?'

'Isn't that enough. I don't want you getting big headed.'

'I won't. And don't stop just because you've come. Finish me off.'

'Say please.'

He smiled. 'You and I are very alike, Danielle,' he said. 'We both like control.'

'Don't we,' she said, and lifted herself up until his cock nearly came out of her.

'No.' he said.

'Ask me nicely.'

'Don't stop.' He saw her face, and felt her withdraw further. 'Please.'

'Pretty please.'

'You bitch. Pretty please, then.'

As he said it, she slid back down the length of his shaft, and began to bounce up and down again on it.

She saw him close his eyes in pleasure and he pushed up as hard as he could until, after a moment or two, she felt the hot liquid jet out of him again and splash into her love tunnel.

She dropped down beside him, panting from exertion. 'Now you give me a cigarette,' she said. 'And light it for me.'

He did as she told him and they shared it, lying together in Danielle's marriage bed, with the sheets damp from their sexual exertions.

'So are we going out tonight?' he asked eventually.

'Yes. But I'll have to be back here by ten. What's the time now?'

'Almost four. Shall we have a drink, then an early dinner? I know several reasonable places in Clapham.'

'That sounds fine. But I'll need a shower first.'

'Me too. Shall we share one.'

'It'll be a bit of a tight squeeze.'

'I like tight squeezes with you.'

'Come on then,' said Danielle, and she jumped up and tugged Laurence to his feet and led him to the bathroom.

They played together under the shower like two children, soaping each other's most intimate and sensitive parts and rinsing the soap off until they could bear it no longer, and they coupled once more under the warm spray.

Afterwards, Laurence put his clothes back on and Danielle chose her outfit for the evening.

She got dressed in front of him in the bedroom in a see-through navy blue bra and matching briefs – which made the nest of curly blonde hair that covered her pubis look dark and mysterious – a navy blue suspender belt and navy blue seamed stockings. On top she wore a similarly coloured dress, cut low at the front. She finished the outfit off with dark blue shoes.

As she dressed herself she had to constantly stop Laurence trying to undress her again.

'You're driving me mad,' he said, as she posed round the room each time she covered herself with a garment. Stretching and bending to show her sexy figure and undies off to their best advantage and caressing herself as she slowly and seductively put them on.

'You wanted to watch. If you can't handle it, go downstairs,' she said.

'I can't bear to see your beautiful body being covered up. Especially as I won't be seeing you take them off.'

'I know darling,' she said. 'I feel the same about you. And I'll be thinking of you later when my husband helps me undress.'

'Bitch.' said Laurence.

'Aren't I?' And she put out her tongue at him.

Eventually she was fully clothed and when her hair and make-up was to her satisfaction, she said, 'I'm ready now.'

'I'll go and get the car,' said Laurence.

'Don't let the whole world see,' said Danielle, getting a lightweight coat from the wardrobe. 'God knows what the neighbours will think. Especially as you've been here all afternoon.'

'I bet no one even noticed,' said Laurence, and jingling his car keys he went downstairs and out through the front door.

16

Laurence took her to a wine bar in Lavender Hill where he ordered champagne. When the bottle arrived he excused himself in order to phone the restaurant to book a table.

When he returned he said, 'I called a friend of mine. He wants to join us. Do you mind?'

'Not at all,' said Danielle. 'The more the merrier.'

'I hoped you'd say that,' said Laurence.

'But remember. I must be home by ten. I am a married woman after all.'

'I shall deliver you to your door before the appointed hour. I'd hate for you to turn into a pumpkin, like Cinderella.'

'I think that was her coach,' said Danielle, with a giggle. 'And I left my glass slippers at home tonight.' She loved champagne, but it always made her act in a silly way.

They arrived at the Thai restaurant which was very trendy and expensive, just before seven. The waiter led them to a table at the back, set for three, and Laurence immediately ordered another bottle of Moet.

'I'll get drunk,' protested Danielle.

'Who cares? The night is young, and you're so beautiful.'

'What time is your friend coming?' asked Danielle, ignoring the compliment.

'He should be here now. In fact here he comes,' said Laurence.

Danielle looked over towards the door where an extremely fat man of about fifty was handing his coat to the waiter.

'Charles,' Laurence hailed him. 'Over here.'

'Larry. How are you? And this must be the lovely Danielle,' said the man. 'And you weren't lying. She *is* lovely.'

He took Danielle's hand and kissed it.

'Danielle, Charles. Charles, Danielle,' said Laurence.

'How do you do?' said Danielle.

'Never better,' replied Charles. 'And champagne. Laurence you'll spoil me.'

'I always try to spoil my friends,' said Laurence. 'Come and sit down.'

Charles took a seat and said, 'I've heard this place is marvellous. The chef's supposed to be a genius.'

'It's not bad,' said Laurence. 'And as it's both yours and Danielle's first time here, may I order for all of us?'

'Of course,' said Charles.

Danielle nodded.

Laurence called the waiter over and asked for chicken satay and king prawn stuffed with crab for starters. For the entrée he ordered seafood, steak in a Thai sauce, chicken with chilli, and rice and noodles, to be accompanied by two bottles of white burgundy.

Once the ordering was done, he lit a cigarette, sat back and said, 'I do love introducing people to each other. Special people. People with a lot in common.'

'Flattery will get you everywhere, eh Danielle?' said Charles, as he too helped himself to a cigarette and lit it. 'Now what exactly is it that you do?'

I wonder what *we're* supposed to have in common, thought Danielle. I really must ask Laurence later.

'I'm a housewife,' she explained.

'A night away from hubby, is it?' said Charles jocularly, but she noticed the look he gave Laurence.

'That's right,' she replied. 'A night off from the cooking.'

Just then the starters arrived and they helped themselves.

After they'd finished eating, and coffees had been served, Danielle said to Laurence, 'It's getting late. I'm afraid I'll have to be going in a few minutes.'

'So soon,' said Charles. 'That's a shame. I thought we might go on somewhere.'

Laurence shrugged. 'We'll have to make it another time old chap. Domesticity calls.'

Danielle smiled sweetly, although she could have kicked him.

Laurence called for the bill and when it arrived Charles insisted on paying. Laurence made only a weak attempt to dissuade him.

'Listen folks,' said Charles, as they parted on the doorstep of the restaurant. 'We really must do this again. And Danielle, make sure you can get a longer pass the next time and we'll really paint the town.'

'I'll try,' she said, linking arms with Laurence as they walked together to his car.

'Who *was* that?' she asked as they went.

'A very rich and powerful man,' he replied. 'Someone to have firmly on your side. And he liked you. I could tell.'

So could I, thought Danielle. At least if the way he kept rubbing his leg up against mine all through dinner meant anything.

Laurence drove her straight home and she was relieved to see that Nigel's car wasn't parked outside when she was dropped off.

'I'll be in touch soon,' said Laurence.

'If you want,' said Danielle in reply. 'But don't just turn up on the doorstep again.'

'I won't. Good night.' He leant over and kissed her on the cheek.

Danielle got out of the car and walked up the path to the front door.

Less than half an hour later Nigel let himself in. He walked into the living room where Danielle was sitting on the sofa watching TV.

'You still up?' he asked.

'I decided to wait for you.'

'Where did the roses come from?' he asked, looking at the flowers she'd rearranged which were now sitting in the vase on the centre of the sideboard.

'I saw them at the shops this morning and couldn't resist them,' Danielle answered. 'I bought them for my favourite man.'

'And you're all dressed up,' her husband said. 'What's the occasion?'

'Once again, for my favourite man. Would you prefer I was in bed with a cup of Horlicks and wearing a winceyette nightie?'

'No,' replied Nigel. 'It's just that I'm not used to roses, and coming home to find you waiting in your best dress.'

'And my best underwear.'

'Is that right?'

'Wouldn't you like to find out?'

Nigel dropped his briefcase on the floor and joined Danielle on the sofa.

'I've decided we should bring back the excitement to our marriage,' she explained.

'You're certainly doing that,' he said, thinking of their lovemaking in the open air the previous weekend. 'Now what was that you said about your best underwear?'

They kissed and Nigel slid his hand up the inside of Danielle's thighs. She parted her legs and allowed his fingers to explore her stocking tops, the fastenings of her suspenders, her bare thighs and the heat where her legs met.

'You're wet,' he said.

'I've been thinking about you all day,' she replied. 'Now why don't you kiss me like a husband.'

He did just that and she responded with her tongue and teeth, biting at *his* tongue and lips.

Nigel pushed the skirt of her dress up to her waist and looked down between her legs. 'I love those panties,' he said.

'I know you do, that's why I wore them.'

'But I prefer them off,' he said.

'Then do it darling.'

He tugged them off her, stuck his face into the wet gusset and breathed in the perfume of her cunt.

She moved closer and kissed him through the material, making them wetter still with her saliva.

'Now kiss my other lips,' she breathed.

Nigel knelt between her open legs and pushed his face into the fragrant hairy dampness between her thighs. He sucked the skin of her quim up into his mouth and gently chewed at it until she cried out in ecstasy. Then he pushed his tongue as deep inside as he could reach and licked round her insides as if it were an ice-cream cone.

'Fuck me,' she cried. 'Here. Now.'

He stood and tore off his clothes until he stood naked in front of her with his penis hard and rigid.

Danielle slid down onto the carpet and lay with her legs wide open. Nigel dropped on top of her and penetrated her cunt with one hard thrust.

She cried out again as he started rogering her pussy with his organ.

He screwed her as hard as he could and she cried for him to fuck her harder, until with a banshee-like wail she came onto his prick and he shot his load inside her, to join that of Laurence's from earlier.

Please God, don't let me get pregnant this week, she thought, I'd have the Devil's own job working out who the father is.

17

After that, Danielle's life once again returned to normal for a few days, but the following Wednesday at the telephone rang.

'Hello Danielle,' said a voice she recognised as Laurence's. 'Can you talk?'

'Yes. But you really shouldn't phone here.'

'I needed to talk to you. How are you?'

'Very well. How are you?'

'Fine. Are you free tomorrow evening?'

As a matter of fact she was. Nigel had disappeared to yet another sales conference – this time in Glasgow – and wasn't due back until Saturday morning.

'I might be,' she replied. 'Why?'

'I thought we could get together. Come round to my place for a few drinks.'

And the rest, thought Danielle.

'I don't know . . .' she said.

'I'll get a gourmet meal sent in. We could have a good time.'

Danielle thought about it for a further thirty seconds. She could feel a tickle of horniness in her belly, and it *would* be better than spending another night alone in front of the TV set.

'All right,' she said. 'What time?'

'About seven.'

'I'll be there,' said Danielle. 'But I don't have your address.'

Laurence dictated it to her, and she copied it down on a sheet of paper.

'Until tomorrow,' he said, and they both hung up.

The next afternoon Danielle prepared for her date with care. The feeling of horniness had grown since the phone call the previous day and she was looking forward to sating it with Laurence.

She took a long, hot bath and painted her finger and toenails a deep scarlet. Then she did her hair and put on her make-up, with plenty of mascara round the eyes and a thick layer of lipstick that matched her nail polish.

Then she chose what she was going to wear. She opted for basic black again from the skin outwards: a black uplift bra; little black knickers with an inset of lace in the front to show off her pubic hair; a black suspender belt; seamed black fishnet stockings; a short black silk dress, cut staggeringly low at the front; and black shoes with very high heels. By six-thirty she was ready, and pulled on a light black coat and got into her Golf to make the short journey from Streatham to Clapham.

She knocked on the door of Laurence's flat at exactly five past seven.

He came to the door dressed in black trousers and a white shirt.

'You look ravishing, darling,' he said after he had kissed her on the cheek and taken her coat and hung it up. 'Come on through.'

He led her into a large living room that was dimly lit and furnished with a three piece suite, bookshelves, a sideboard and a dining table set with a white table-cloth and places for two.

'Sit down,' he invited her, and she chose one of the armchairs. 'A cocktail?'

'I'd love one.'

'Name your poison.'

'A martini cocktail. With a twist.'

'Coming right up.'

He went over to the cocktail cabinet in the corner of the room and got busy mixing Danielle's drink.

'Dinner is in the oven. I go to a very good firm who bring everything. I'm afraid I don't have the time or patience to cook.'

'That's fine,' said Danielle as she accepted the glass from him.

'When we've had a drink, I'll serve the food.'

'Whenever you're ready,' she replied.

The dinner was indeed delightful. They had watercress soup to start, then duck in a gooseberry sauce, with tiny roast potatoes and mixed vegetables, and a delicious lemon sorbet for sweet. With it Laurence served a fine rosé wine.

After he'd cleared the table and put the dishes into the dishwasher, he brought out freshly made coffee and the brandy bottle.

Danielle sat in her armchair feeling relaxed and well fed, and Laurence said, 'Charles might be calling in later.'

'Is that right?' said Danielle.

'Yes. I told him you were coming and he begged to see you again. He's really taken a shine to you.'

'What are you up to Laurence?' asked Danielle.

'What *do* you mean? He's a very nice bloke. It would do you no harm at all to get to know him better.'

'How much better?'

'That's up to you.'

'But he's so fat.'

'And so rich.'

At ten o'clock the front door bell rang.

'That'll be him now,' said Laurence, as he got to his feet to answer it. 'Now be nice.'

'I always am,' replied Danielle. She checked her make-up in her mirror and added an extra layer of lipstick. After all, she thought, he is rich.

Laurence led Charles into the room and said, 'I was right. It is Charles. Charles you remember Danielle, don't you?'

'How could I forget?' asked the fat man, and shook Danielle's hand.

She smiled up at him from where she was sitting.

'A drink, Charles?' asked Laurence.

'As long as I'm not interrupting anything.'

'Of course not.'

'Then I'll join you in a brandy.'

Laurence got another glass, poured Charles a stiff measure and replenished both his own and Danielle's drink.

Charles took his glass, sat down on the other sofa and lit a cigarette.

'It's so pleasant to see you again, Danielle. I did enjoy our dinner the other night,' he said.

'So did I,' she said, and slightly under the influence of the alcohol she'd drunk that night, she crossed her legs, giving Charles a flash of her stocking tops.

She could see that Charles enjoyed the view and she

decided that it would be good sport to tease him some more.

'Laurence has been telling me about you,' she said. 'He told me you're very rich.'

Charles smiled. 'Absolutely loaded,' he said. 'I run a business making car parts. I don't know about the recession, but my firm's never been busier. I suppose people are keeping their old cars on the road longer.'

'It sounds fascinating,' said Danielle.

'It's pretty boring really. But it pays the rent and buys the occasional Thai dinner.'

Danielle crossed her legs again, and she saw Charles's eyes move to look at her thighs. She knew that with very little effort she could have him in her power – at least until he had shot his load – and the knowledge made her smile to herself. Stupid man, she thought. So full of himself and his business and his money, but what I've got between my legs can cut him down to size in a second.

In fact she felt rather sorry for him and began to like him more than she had previously.

She saw Laurence looking as well and knew that he knew what she was doing.

She smiled at him and he smiled back. Suddenly she understood that this had been part of his plan all along. Although she realised that he was using her, she really didn't care.

Laurence stood up and went to pour more drinks. As he gave Danielle hers, he sat on the arm of the sofa next to her. She looked up at him and he began to play with the ends of her hair.

He wants to fuck me, she thought. Then she looked at Charles and realised that Laurence wanted him to fuck her as well. A threesome. She shivered at the thought. She'd almost had one with Dave and Johnny at the garage when she'd been driving to Southampton, but it had been slightly different; Dave and Johnny hadn't watched each other fuck her. But here and now she assumed that Laurence wanted all three of them in bed at the same time.

She smiled up at Laurence and touched his hand with hers.

What the hell, she thought. There was a first time for everything and Charles didn't look so bad after a few brandies.

She crossed her legs again, but this time she let her skirt ride up her legs until the tops of her stockings were exposed. Charles's eyes almost popped out of their sockets.

She smiled over at him too, and opened her legs so that he had a clear view of her naked thighs, her suspenders, and the black lace gusset of her panties.

He stared between her legs as if mesmerised and she felt her pussy oozing a sticky wetness as she displayed herself for him.

Laurence stood up and said, 'Shall we go to the bedroom?' He put out his hand for Danielle to take.

She did so and he pulled her to her feet.

'Coming Charlie?' he said.

Charles lumbered to his feet and, glass in hand, followed Danielle and Laurence into the bedroom.

The bedroom was large and dim and the room was dominated by the huge bed that seemed to take up at least sixty percent of the floor space. It was covered in a black bedspread and the sheets and pillowcases were made of black satin. One wall of the room was completely covered in smoked mirrored glass and above the bed, the ceiling was mirrored also.

'I want you to fuck Charles while I watch,' said Laurence. 'I've given you to him for the evening.'

'Is that right?' asked Danielle. 'Am I your property now to be given away when you want? Like a piece of meat?'

Laurence nodded, and Danielle once again felt that familiar thrill of lust in her loins.

Right, she thought, if I'm just a piece of meat, I'll enjoy it. And I'll make you jealous into the bargain, you bastard.

Laurence moved to the corner of the room and sat on an upright armchair covered in maroon velvet. Danielle went over to Charles and said, 'It looks like I belong to you tonight. So you can do what you want with me.' She put her hand between his legs, and felt his erection through his trousers.

'What do you want me to do?' she asked. 'I'll do anything you want, I promise.'

Charles swallowed hard and licked his lips, then finished his brandy in one gulp and said, 'Undress me.'

Danielle slid his suit jacket off his shoulders and dropped it on the floor. Then she undid his tie and threw it on top of his jacket, and began to unbutton his shirt. His bare chest was thick with hair and his breasts were almost as big as Danielle's own, but somehow the mat of black hair on them made them irresistibly sexy to her. His nipples were purple with blood and she sucked first one, then the other between her lips and tweaked them with her tongue.

She pulled his shirt out of his trousers and tugged it off, so that Charles was naked to the waist. The mat of hair on his body went across his shoulders and down his back, disappearing into the waistband of his suit pants. She stood behind him and ran her hands down his spine, gently tugging at his pelt with her scarlet fingertips as she went.

'You're so *hairy*,' she said.

'Do you mind?' asked Charles.

'Not at all, On the contrary. I like it.' Then looking at Laurence, 'No,' she said. 'In fact, I love it.'

Laurence sat passively in the corner and looked on.

Danielle went round to face Charles again and undid the button at the top of the waistband of his trousers. Then she knelt before him and removed first one shoe and sock, then the other. Still kneeling, she pulled down the zip of his fly and allowed his trousers to drop to the floor. Charles's gut was huge, but so was the prick sticking through the material of his boxer shorts, and the hair that covered his body covered both legs as well. Danielle gently pulled down his underpants to allow his penis freedom. It was long and thick with a bend in the middle, and a huge fat uncircumcised knob at the end, and it poked from a mass of pubic hair so thick and black it was like the fur of a bear.

Danielle took hold of his prick and gently kissed the end, then she looked up and said, 'What now?'

'Stand up,' said Charles, his voice sounding deep and throaty.

Danielle did as he told her.

He took her in his arms and kissed her on the mouth. She responded immediately and wrapped her arms and one leg around his nakedness.

'Strip for me,' he said.

She smiled and pulled up the skirt of her dress. Slowly she undid the suspenders that fastened her right stocking, kicked off her right shoe, rolled the stocking down and

114

tugged it off the ends of her toes. Then she draped it over Charles's hard prick. She did the same with her left shoe and stocking, and then turned round, looking over her shoulder to ask Charles to unzip her dress. Which he did. She allowed her dress to fall to the floor and stepped out of it, leaving her standing in only bra, panties and suspender belt. She undid the fastenings of the belt and flicked it across the room where it fell onto Laurence's lap. Then Danielle undid the snaps on her bra and, bending forward, allowed the straps to slide off her shoulders. Holding the material to her chest with one hand, she stood upright before dropping the garment to the floor and allowing her breasts to swing free in front of the two men's eyes.

Then finally, and terribly slowly, she eased her tight black panties over her hips and down her legs, until they too dropped to the floor, allowing her to daintily step out of the flimsy undergarments and stand stark naked in front of Charles and Laurence.

She held her arms up at shoulder height and twirled round, showing every inch of her nude body to them.

'Do you like me, Charles?' she asked. 'Am I as good looking as you thought I'd be?'

Charles nodded, held open his arms, and within a second she was rubbing her naked breasts against the thick, wiry hair that coated his chest. She'd never been so close to such a hairy man and it excited her terribly, so much so that the juice from her pussy was bubbling hotly from between the lips of her cunny and rolling slowly and sensuously down her thighs.

Charles picked her up in his strong arms and carried her over to the bed. He laid her gently on her back, onto the coolness of the bedspread, then lay next to her. His great bulk loomed over her and she felt tiny and feminine as he pulled her into his arms and engulfed her in the warmth of his huge hairy body.

He leaned down and covered her mouth with his and they French kissed enthusiastically. Danielle felt Charles's hands move to her breasts and cup first one, then the other in his palm, and gently roll her nipples between his fingers and thumbs. The sensation ran down from her tits to her cunt like a slow electric shock and she opened her legs instinctively.

Charles's mouth moved down to her neck and she looked over his shoulder into the shadows at the corner of the room where Laurence was still sitting and watching. She saw the gleam of his eyes in the darkness, as Charles's mouth bit at the smooth skin of her breasts, and she cried out half in pain and half in pleasure as she forgot all about Laurence, her mind returning to her new lover. His mighty paws went down to her thighs and she felt his fat fingers in the slippery mess around the entrance to her crack. Then they slid inside her love tunnel and she threw back her head in pleasure as he opened her up with them.

Then they moved up to the crack of her arse and, still slick and slippery with her cunt juice, Charles began to poke his forefinger into her back passage.

How Danielle loved that feeling. It reminded her of the afternoon with Dave in his caravan, and the wonderful orgasm she'd had as he screwed her in the arsehole for the first time. The feeling was exactly the same. First there was the long stab of pain as the opening of her anus was stretched almost to bursting point, and then, just like before, the pain turned miraculously to pleasure. Danielle wriggled on the end of Charles's finger like a fish on a hook, as he pushed his digit further and further inside her. She loved the feeling and wanted more. Lots more.

'Bugger me,' she said to Charles. 'Screw me. Fuck me there. Stick your fat prick up my arse.'

Charles smiled down at her. 'All in good time,' he said. 'Have patience my lovely.'

'Please,' she begged. 'I love it in there.'

'I thought you would,' said Charles. 'I said that to Laurence earlier when we arranged this. But first, I want you to cover my cock with your lovely, smelly cunt cream, so that I can slide all the way up your arsehole easily.'

'Go on then,' said Danielle. 'But be quick. I need your cock in my bum like I've never needed anything before.'

In a trice he pushed her flat on her back and was between her legs. She felt his cock push open the lips of her cunt and enter her. It slid smoothly up the inside of her love tunnel and she grabbed his fur with both hands and tugged him down on top of her. But he was determined to do as she wanted and bum-fuck her. As soon as his cock was all the way up into her pussy, he pulled it out, turned her roughly onto her front, and forced his cock into her bottom. She bit at the edge of the pillow in agony as her tender anus was assaulted by his solid meat. Then, as always seemed to happen, the agony became ecstasy and, slowly but surely, an inch at a time, he pushed his penis all the way into her arse.

It seemed to take forever for his monstrous organ to penetrate, but it was worth it. When it was completely in – and Danielle could feel his balls resting on the cheeks of her bottom – Charles began to move his cock slowly up and down, much to Danielle's delight.

She could hear his hoarse breathing and feel the weight

of him on her back and she loved every ounce of pressure he was exerting on to her.

'Shoot me,' she cried. 'Shoot me for Christ's sake. I want your come.'

She knew that Charles was trying to prolong the fuck, but she wanted his jism inside her, and inside her right away. She pushed her arse up into his groin and the length of his cock seemed to enter an even more pleasurable section of her body. Suddenly she felt herself lose control as she came on to Charles's organ with a howl of sheer delight.

That was all he was waiting for. As she climaxed noisily, he pumped hard at her slim body and felt his own spasm begin. Then he burst into her arse as if the sensation would never end.

18

Danielle felt Charles's huge bulk collapse on top of her a
he tried to catch his breath, and she felt his cock soften
inside her back passage until eventually he pulled out and
rolled over, puffing and blowing on the bed next to her.

'Was that good?' she asked.

'Wonderful,' panted Charles.

She got off the bed and said to Laurence, 'I want to
wash him. Where's the bathroom?'

Laurence remained where he was and pointed to an
almost invisible door in the wall next to him.

In the bathroom she found a flannel which she soaked
in warm water and took it, and a soft towel, back to Charles.
She carefully washed his cock, paying special attention to
the tender area beneath his foreskin, and within a minute
she felt the member beginning to grow in her hand. When
she was sure it was clean, she dabbed it dry with the towel
and covered the hardening knob with her lips, sucking at
the hole. Within another minute his love rod was firm and
hard in her mouth.

She sat up and said to Charles, 'I want you to fuck me
in my cunt now.'

'I don't know if I've got the strength,' he replied.

'Don't worry, I'll do all the work,' said Danielle.

119

'You just lie back and enjoy it.'

She climbed aboard his obese body, and perched on top of his cock, allowing it to slide right up into her pussy. Then, still sitting upright, she began to gently bounce up and down on Charles's groin.

She could see herself in the mirror that covered one wall and, knowing what she must look like to Laurence, she laughed out loud. There she was, a beautiful young girl, sitting on top of a fat old man fucking the life out of him, and they were both loving every second of it.

She lay down, with her chest on Charles's and her mane of blonde hair cascading across his face, and dug her fingers into the fur on his shoulders. She pumped down onto his cock as hard as she could and she felt him pushing himself up into her.

She rode him harder, closing her legs tightly over his engorged cock and she could hear him breathing faster into her ear as he came close to another orgasm.

'Come on top of me,' she said. 'I want you to crush me.'

They rolled over and Danielle slid off Charles's prick and lay on her back.

Once again he mounted her and she steered his prick back into the wide and wanting hole between her legs.

He began to push his hips at hers and they soon found a rhythm that suited them both. With each thrust she felt the exquisite pleasure that she'd come to love as he strove to shoot his spunk into her once more. She adored the feeling of his weight grinding her into the mattress and she put her feet onto his calves and joined her arms behind his huge bulk, hanging on for dear life as he rammed himself down into her body.

She looked over at Laurence and saw that he had taken his cock out of his trousers and was wanking himself slowly as he watched her and Charles rutting together.

The sight of his lovely cock in his hand drove her almost to distraction, and she called for Charles to ride her harder, which he happily did until she felt she was on a roller coaster ride of pleasure that could only have one destination – total and complete joy.

Charles began to moan and she could feel his balls bouncing between the cheeks of her arse, getting harder and harder with each stroke, as he came closer and closer to his climax.

She reached down with one hand and gently cupped his scrotum, pulling at the hair on his back with the other, and he dug his prick deeper into her until she knew that he was only seconds away from spunking into her once more. Then his whole body stiffened on a down stroke and she ground her clitoris up into his groin, screaming in pleasure as she felt his jism jet into her insides. As Danielle reached her own climax, she dragged his body down to squash hers against the bed, until she felt herself almost lose consciousness with the pleasure of their fuck.

19

They lay together in silence after their mutual come and Danielle felt the sweat running down from Charles's body combine with her own.

They stayed locked in their steamy embrace for a few minutes until Danielle heard his breath deepen as he fell asleep. He seemed to get even heavier then and she could hardly breath for the weight of him. She wriggled out from under his body and lay beside him on the soft bedspread.

Laurence got up from where he'd been sitting and, still with his erect penis poking out from the fly of his trousers, came over to the bed and stood beside Danielle.

She looked up at him. 'Did you like watching?' she said.

He nodded and she reached up with her scarlet tipped fingers and took his cock into her hand.

'Did you make yourself come?' she asked.

He shook his head.

'Then let me.'

She sat up and took his cock into her mouth, where Charles's had been just a few minutes earlier.

Laurence's prick felt and tasted different and she licked and kissed the length of it as he closed his eyes at the beautiful feeling her ministrations gave him.

She sucked as hard as she could, undid the button on his trousers and eased them down until she could free his balls and tickle the back of them. She slid her fingers up into the crease of her arse, until she found his hole, and scratched at it with the nail of her third finger. When he gasped with pleasure she knew that soon she'd be drinking his thick juice. She sucked harder at his prick, and he dug his hands into her hair. She pulled him closer, and she heard him cry out once before he jerked inside her mouth, shooting a thick gout of salty tasting sperm into the back of her throat, which she gulped down like a drowning man being given a drink of sweet spring water.

When his orgasm was over, he staggered back and looked down at her again.

'You're a filthy whore,' he said.

'So are you,' she replied. 'We were made for each other.'

20

Laurence pushed his cock back into his trousers and fastened them, then picked up her dress and threw it at her.

'Put that on, you slut, and get in the other room. I want to talk to you.'

Danielle smiled as she got off the bed and stepped into her dress. Gotcha! she thought.

She left Charles sleeping on the bed and followed Laurence into the living room where he was pouring himself another drink.

'One for me?' she said.

He splashed brandy into a balloon and handed it to her.

'What's the matter?' she asked. 'Didn't I do what you wanted me to?'

He didn't answer.

'Or was it because I enjoyed it too much?'

Once again, no reply.

'It was, wasn't it?'

'Maybe,' acknowledged Laurence.

'I thought you'd get off on it,' she said. 'And you did, didn't you?'

'Maybe,' he said again.

'Course you did. I could tell. And I can tell you're getting off on it again.'

Danielle could clearly see the shape of his cock growing in his trousers again.

'I'll do anything you want me to, darling,' she said. 'Anything at all. You know that.'

Until I decide differently, she thought.

'I thought you wanted me to make Charles think I was enjoying it.'

'And weren't you?'

'Of course not,' she lied. 'You're the only man for me. I'll do anything for you.'

'Anything?' he said.

'I told you. Anything.'

'Lie down then, on the sofa.'

She did as he said and watched him as he stripped naked in front of her.

He really does have a lovely body, and a *beautiful* cock, she thought, as he pulled off his underpants and stood naked in front of her.

And such staying power, she marvelled, because his cock – which she had emptied into her mouth just a few minutes before – was once again hard and erect.

'Pull up your skirt and open your legs, whore,' ordered Laurence.

Danielle loved being talked to like that.

Dirty girl, she thought, as she did as he commanded her. She pulled the skirt of her dress up to her waist and opened her legs as wide as she could, and she saw him staring at the beautiful blonde floss between her thighs, damp and dank from the fuck she'd had with Charles.

Laurence walked over to her and lay on top of her supine body, supporting himself above her on his rigid arms. Without any preliminaries, like kissing or caressing,

126

he sunk his shaft deep into her flesh, so brutally that even though she was wet and open she felt a stab of pain in her belly.

'Bastard,' she said between clenched teeth, as he started to pound at her, all the time holding himself above her, and staring down into her face.

She writhed under the battering he was giving her, but he refused to relent.

'Stop it, you're hurting me,' she pleaded. 'Stop it now.'

'When I'm ready,' he panted, beating at her body harder. Suddenly, as it always seemed to for her, the pain turned to something else akin to pleasure, and she wanted him to pound her even harder, until he killed her with his fucking.

She looked up at his face, and saw it begin to twist with pleasure, and she rammed herself up into his body with a force that matched his own, until, with a strangled cry, he emptied his seed into her abdomen.

'Don't stop, you fucker,' she cried. 'Don't you dare stop.'

But before she could come, he pulled straight out of her and began to get dressed.

'Is that it?' she said. 'Is that all, you bastard?'

'If you want more,' he said, as he slipped into his shirt, 'do it yourself.'

'I'll do a better job,' she said, and found her cunt with the fingers of her right hand. She slid them inside until they touched her clitoris with a jolt of pleasure and slowly she moved her fingers round on the hard gristle, until she felt pleasure flood through her body.

'Much better,' she said.

Her fingers moved faster and she saw Laurence watching her.

The thought of a man seeing her masturbate excited her tremendously and, as her breathing became faster, and her tongue darted across her dry lips, she came onto her own hand with a cry that matched Laurence's earlier sounds of pleasure.

She lay there panting and looked over at him.

'Did you enjoy that?' he asked.

She nodded.

'I think you were right,' he said. 'We *were* made for each other.'

'I'm still horny,' she said. 'Will you come and lick me out?'

Laurence laughed. 'You really are a slag, darling,' he said.

Danielle picked up her glass of brandy that was standing on the carpet next to the sofa and splashed the contents across her cunt. She bit her lip in pain as the fiery liquor burnt into the soft flesh.

'Come on,' she said. 'Come and have a drink on me.'

Laurence came over and knelt down and she moved round so that he could put his head between her legs. He slurped at the mixture of booze and sex-juice in her cunt, and licked deep into her sex until she bucked and cried out and came again straight into his mouth.

21

Danielle arrived home with the milk, feeling sore and used, but satisfied after her night of sex with Laurence and Charles. She parked her car in the front of the house and ducked in, hoping none of the neighbours noticed. She stripped naked in the bathroom and dived into a tub of hot, scented water.

When she'd spent a lazy hour luxuriating in the bath, she got out, dried herself, dressed in cotton undies, a pair of baggy trousers and an old sweater, and made a cup of coffee.

She checked the answer phone, but there were no messages, so she picked the morning paper off the mat and went into the living room to have her drink and catch up on the news.

When she'd finished her coffee, she washed up her cup, wrote out a shopping list, and went to the local supermarket to stock up the larder for Nigel's return the next evening.

She was wandering around the aisles, pushing her trolley, when she heard her name being called.

She looked round and saw Richard Greenstreet, who lived in the house opposite hers and Nigel's, smiling from behind a display of Campbell's soup tins.

He was about thirty-five, tall and dark, and not

unattractive, except for his rather smarmy attitude. He was an advertising copywriter who worked mainly from home. That day he was wearing a pair of tight blue jeans and a pink cotton sweater. He was divorced and lived alone, and was part of the local scene that got together for the occasional party in the winter months, or barbecues in the summer. Although he'd never made an overt pass at Danielle, she'd often caught him eyeing her up speculatively when he thought that she wasn't looking.

'Richard,' she said. 'How are you?'

'Fine. Long time no see. Or at least long time no speak.' She shrugged. 'You know how it is. Nigel's been away a lot lately. And I'm not up on the social scene at the moment.'

'Is that right?' he said. 'I thought just the opposite.'

She frowned. 'I'm sorry,' she said.

'I thought I saw someone calling on you last week with a *very* large bunch of roses. You seemed quite sociable to him. At least, he didn't leave for hours.' Seeing her look, he added, 'Not that I was being nosey. I was working at my desk, and I've moved it into the window to get the best of the sun.'

Danielle's heart was suddenly in her mouth.

Damn Laurence, she thought. I *knew* someone would notice.

'It was just a friend,' she said. Then cursed herself for justifying Laurence's visit.

'A nice friend to bring such a present,' said Richard, and Danielle caught the hint of a leer in his expression.

Not being nosey, she thought. You bloody liar.

'Isn't he?' she said as calmly as she could. 'A business associate of Nigel's.'

'Trying to get to him through the little woman, eh? I'll have to mention that to him next time I see him. If any of my business associates had taken a bunch of roses like that to my wife, when I was married I'd've been very suspicious.'

Danielle could have bitten out her tongue.

'Where is old Nige, by the way?' asked Richard. 'I haven't seen his car around for a few days.'

A right little neighbourhood watcher aren't you? thought Danielle.

'Away on business,' she said. 'He'll be back tomorrow.'

'And I didn't see *your* car last night either,' added her neighbour.

Danielle smiled through gritted teeth.

'I went to visit some friends.'

'I suppose you get lonely with your husband away so much?'

Not lonely enough to invite you round, thought Danielle.

'I'm used to it,' she said sweetly. 'And now I'd better get on, I must get in some supplies for Nigel's homecoming dinner. I do like to make it a special occasion.'

She smiled again, and pushed her trolley past Richard in the direction of the deli counter.

Bastard, she thought as she went.

When she got home she went straight to the drinks cupboard, poured herself an extremely large gin and tonic, and thought about what Richard had said. She wondered if he would mention her gentleman caller to Nigel, and what she could do about preventing it. She had a pretty good idea what her neighbour wanted, and wondered how long she'd have to wait to find out if what she thought was true.

It wasn't long.

Nigel phoned on Friday night and told her he'd be home at about five the following evening. Danielle caught up on her beauty sleep on Friday night and on Saturday began to prepare Nigel's special dinner.

By four o'clock everything was ready and Danielle went upstairs to change. She put on a simple black dress over a black, longline corset with suspenders attached, tiny black net panties and sheer black stockings. On her feet she wore high-heeled black court shoes. As she was putting the finishing touches to her make-up, the doorbell rang.

She wondered if Nigel had forgotten his key and she went down to answer the door. On the doorstep was Richard Greenstreet.

'Danielle,' he said. 'I'm so sorry to disturb you. Is Nigel home yet?'

'No,' replied Danielle, 'but I'm expecting him at any minute. What can I do for you?'

'I know it's a nuisance, but could I borrow some milk? The milkman forgot to call today, and I'm all out. I don't want to go to the shops. I'm on a deadline for some copy, and a dispatch rider's coming for it in an hour. It's one of the problems of being freelance – working at weekends when others are playing.'

The transparency of the excuse was so apparent that Danielle almost laughed, but instead she said, 'Of course Richard, do come in.'

She showed him into the living room and offered him a drink.

'Just a small one,' he said. 'Like I said, duty calls.'

Of course it does, thought Danielle.

'Help yourself.' she said. 'Everything's there, and there's

ice in the bucket. I'll get you a pint of milk out of the fridge. I won't be a moment.'

When she was in the kitchen she heard Nigel's key in the front door, and then voices as he found Richard in the living room.

Danielle went in with the milk, as Richard was explaining the reason for his visit.

'Hello, darling,' she said to Nigel as she walked in. He was standing in the middle of the room holding a huge bunch of red roses, just like the ones Laurence had bought her the previous week, the remains of which were still in the vase on the sideboard.

'Listen,' said Richard, as he gulped at the scotch on the rocks he'd made himself. 'I won't disturb your reunion.'

'No problem,' said Nigel. 'Have another drink.'

'No I really mustn't,' said Richard, then, 'I say, more roses. You are a lucky girl Danielle. Getting two beautiful bouquets like that within a few days.'

'Not guilty. Well, not for that lot anyway.' Nigel said, indicating the vase. 'Danielle bought them for me. So I was the lucky one there. I'm just returning the compliment with these.'

Richard took the bottle of milk from Danielle's hand and said, 'You certainly are the lucky one, old boy. I *do* envy you. Well I really must be going. I'm sure I'll be seeing you two again sooner or later.'

Danielle saw the triumphant look he gave her as Nigel showed him to the door and she knew it would be sooner rather than later in her case.

Damn it, she thought. Another fine mess I've got myself into.

22

'Nice chap,' said Nigel as he came back into the living room.

Sure, thought Danielle. In a pig's ear. He wants your wife on her back, Sonny, and unfortunately it looks as if he might get her.

'Isn't he?' she said.

'Come here,' said Nigel, 'and give me a hug. I've missed you.'

'I've missed you too,' said Danielle and went into his arms, temporarily putting the problem of Richard to the back of her mind.

Nigel ran his hands over her body and said, 'What are you wearing?'

'My corset.'

'It feels very constrictive,' he said.

'That's how I like it,' she replied. 'Tight and hard. Like your cock.'

'You are getting to be a filthy girl,' he said.

'Don't you like it?'

'On the contrary, I love it.'

'Good,' she said. 'Now control yourself. Have a drink. Dinner's nearly ready, and we've got the whole night in front of us.'

'I'm looking forward to it,' replied Nigel.

The food that Danielle had prepared was excellent, and they had a long and leisurely meal, followed by Irish coffees in the living room with The Carpenters greatest hits playing softly on the stereo in the background.

Danielle and Nigel sat next to each other on the sofa and Nigel gently ran his hand up one of his wife's thighs, feeling the fastener of her suspender through the thin material of her dress.

'You look very beautiful tonight,' he said.

'Thank you, kind sir.'

'That dress suits you. It brings out the best in your figure.'

'I think the corset might have something to do with that.'

'Oh yes, the corset, I'd forgotten about that,' he lied.

'Liar,' she said.

He grinned. 'You're right. I am.'

'Do you want to see it?' she asked.

He nodded.

She stood up, went over to the record player, took off The Carpenters album, and substituted it for one by Luther Vandross. As his warm tones filled the room seductively, she began to move to the music and reached up and unfastened the zip at the back of her dress and pulled it down slowly. As the music continued she pushed the garment off her shoulders and let it drop to the floor where she stepped out of it.

She looked magnificent in the soft light from the single lamp in the room. In its warm glow she stood in front of her husband gently rolling her hips in time to the music that oozed out of the speakers.

Her long legs were shown off to their best advantage in the sheer black stockings that reflected the glow from the bulb, then dramatically stopped halfway up her creamy thighs, so that the skin appeared even whiter in the contrast to her hose, and the thin black line of the suspenders that kept the stockings fastened. Her brief panties barely concealed the swell of her pubis and stray blonde hairs escaped the tight elastic at the legs. Her corset cruelly bound the flesh of her hips and waist and pushed the twin orbs of her breasts upwards. The net material clearly showed the raspberry pink colour of her nipples, that were fighting hard to escape from the constraint of the material.

Nigel could hardly breath as he watched his wife exhibit herself to him.

'Y-You look gorgeous,' he stammered.

She smiled saucily. 'And it's all for you, darling,' she said. Tonight, at least, she thought. But tomorrow, who knows? 'Come and dance with me.'

He got to his feet and went into her arms. Her perfume overpowered his senses and the feel of her body in his embrace was overtly sexual.

They danced together for a minute or two before he kissed her on the lips, and they stood together in the centre of the room, swaying slightly to the hypnotic beat of the music as Nigel ran his hands over his wife's body. He felt his organ grow between his legs and push into the soft flesh of her belly.

'That's nice,' said Danielle, and pushed closer to him, rotating her hips against his cock.

He slid his hands down the elasticated back of her corset and over her buttocks – which he gripped tightly – and pulled her even closer if that were possible.

She ground her groin into his and he led her back to the sofa where they collapsed together and began to kiss again.

Danielle wrestled off Nigel's jacket and undid his tie and pulled it off as he kissed and caressed her. One of his shirt buttons popped as she hastily undid it and tugged it out of his trousers. Then she reached for the buckle on his belt and unfastened it, followed by the button at the top of his trousers, and the zip at the fly. He moved around so that she could reach inside and she pulled his cock from out of his clothes, holding it in her hand. She put her head down and breathed onto the knob at the end, then licked round it, leaving a trail of saliva behind her tongue.

She sat up and kissed him on the mouth again and, still holding his cock with her fingers, gently began to run the ball of her thumb over the helmet, using her spit as lubrication.

Nigel nearly fainted at the sensation.

'That is beautiful,' he said between kisses.

She slid her thumbnail into his hole and he cried out with pleasure.

'My God,' he said. 'What are you doing?'

'Sshh,' she whispered, and closed her mouth onto his, sliding her thumbnail in a little deeper.

Nigel felt sweat breaking out on his forehead at the sensation and put his hand high on Danielle's thigh above her stocking tops. As she opened her legs he pushed his hand up to the wet crotch of her panties, then under the elastic, through the tight curls that covered her mons, and into the swamp of juice that she'd secreted to receive his love rod.

'Why are you so horny?' he asked.

'I love you Nigel, that's why,' she said back.

'I want you now,' he said. 'On the floor.'

'Come on then,' she said, dragging him off the sofa.

He hopped from one foot to the other as he tore his trousers and underpants off and quickly joined Danielle on the carpet, literally ripping the tiny panties she was wearing off her hips. Without removing her corset or stockings, he mounted her and pushed his cock into her hot, wet, welcoming slit.

He drove his cock into her like a hammer and she took every inch of him up to his balls.

Danielle pulled his head down and covered his face with kisses as he moved on top of her, and she pushed herself up against his bollocks.

He loved the feel of her underwear against his naked skin, especially the nylon of her stockings as she entwined her legs around his and scraped the material up his thighs and over his bottom in her contortions to get more of his flesh inside her.

'Spunk me,' she cried. 'Fill me with it.'

As she called for her husband to fill her crevice with his seed, he pushed harder and faster against her, and as he banged his body against hers, he felt as if his scrotum was going to explode. Finally, with a scream, he let loose his come into her. She felt the heat of it burn her womb, and succumbed to the beginning of a beautiful orgasm that seemed to sweep through her body like a tidal wave, leaving her weak and exhausted under the body of her husband, with her back burning from the friction of the carpet against it.

Shag pile, she thought, as she gave in to the sensation and let it carry her to heaven.

23

They lay together after their sex, until Danielle dragged herself to her feet. She found the remains of her knickers where Nigel had tossed them, and held them up. The crotch had been torn out of them, and she threw them carelessly into the waste-paper bin by the fireplace. She struggled into her dress and looked down at her husband lying exhausted at her feet.

She smiled and touched him with one nylon-clad toe.

'Are you still alive?' she asked.

He opened one eye and regarded her through it. 'Barely,' he replied.

'More coffee?' she said.

'You're a wonderful woman.'

'I know,' she replied, going into the kitchen to put the coffee pot back on the burner.

When she came back with two steaming mugs, Nigel had managed to drag himself into his boxer shorts and back onto the sofa. He took his mug from her gratefully and said, 'I don't know what's come over you lately, Danielle. But I love it.'

I wonder if you would, if you really knew, she thought.

'Like I told you before, I'm just trying to put some of the magic back into our marriage,' she said.

'Well you're succeeding,' said Nigel.

Rather sadly, she realised that she was, but at what cost?

She leaned over and kissed him on the cheek. 'I'm about ready for bed,' she said. 'You've exhausted me. Are you coming?'

He nodded and together they took their drinks up to the bedroom.

The rest of the weekend passed quietly enough and bright and early on Monday morning, Nigel got into his car and drove to his office.

All the way there, he was thinking about his wife and her new found interest in sex, and all day he became more and more excited.

Meanwhile at home, Danielle had washed up the breakfast things and been to the shops. At around noon, she made herself a sandwich and a pot of coffee, and settled down with a copy of her favourite magazine in front of the twelve o'clock news on the TV.

At five past exactly, the front doorbell rang.

Damn, she thought. Who the hell is this now?

She flung down the magazine and went to the door. Richard Greenstreet was standing on the doorstep carrying a pint of milk.

'Richard,' she said. 'I wasn't expecting you.'

I'd forgotten all about you, in fact, she thought. But here you are, turning up again like a bad penny.

'Danielle,' he greeted her. 'I came to give you back the milk I borrowed.'

'You shouldn't have bothered, Richard,' said Danielle. 'Anytime would have done.'

'But if you return a favour promptly, you can always ask again,' he said with a smile.

She looked him up and down. That day he was wearing tight white pants and a lemon yellow sweater, and didn't look half bad.

He must have taken some trouble with his appearance this morning, thought Danielle. And smiled to herself. I wonder why?

Richard sniffed the air. 'Is that fresh coffee I smell?' he asked.

'It is. I was just having some lunch.'

If she thought that that was going to get rid of him, she was wrong.

'Sounds delightful,' he said. 'I don't suppose I could beg a cup. Mine's all instant these days. Since my wife left. You know how it is? The joys of bachelorhood.'

He stood on the doorstep like a dog who'd forgotten where he'd buried his favourite bone, and Danielle was tempted for a moment to close the door in his face. But she relented. A few weeks ago, she wouldn't have. But times had changed, and so had she, and she had to admit that he *really* didn't look half bad. She was also interested to see in what way his approach towards her, that she knew he would make, would come.

'I can imagine,' she said, and opened the door all the way. 'Come on in. I think I can squeeze half a cup out of the pot.'

He brushed past her closely and she could smell his aftershave. Pathetic, she thought. Men!

'Go into the living room,' she said. 'I'll get your coffee. Would you like something to eat? A sandwich?'

'That would be great.'

'Chicken salad?'

'Fine.'

For chicken shit, she thought.

She took the bottle of milk that he was holding, went into the kitchen and quickly prepared a sandwich from the remains of the makings of her own, and poured him a cup of coffee.

She went back into the hall and called out. 'Black or white?'

'White,' he replied through the living room door. 'One sugar.'

She went back to the kitchen and added cream and sugar to his cup. Then she took it, with the sandwich, into the living room, where Richard was sitting on the sofa, watching the end of the news. She gave him the plate, and cup and saucer, and sat down opposite him in an armchair.

'You look very sporty this afternoon,' said Richard.

Danielle was wearing a turquoise and purple shell-suit, with towelling socks and trainers. Underneath she had on plain white cotton undies.

'Just shopping and housework gear,' she replied.

'I must say it's a bit of a change from what you were wearing the other day,' he said.

'That was different. A special occasion.'

'I thought you looked gorgeous, if you don't mind me saying so.'

'Not at all. I'm flattered,' she said. And she was a bit, although she knew very well where the conversation was leading.

'Did you have a good evening?' he asked, finishing the last bite of his sandwich and sitting back in the sofa, cup in hand.

'It was wonderful,' said Danielle.

'I wish I had a wife to welcome me back when I get home from a business trip.'

'Perhaps you should get married again.'

He shook his head. 'It's a case of once bitten, I'm afraid. And besides, my wife wasn't a patch on you. Not in the looks or the cooking department. That food smelled delicious on Saturday.'

'Any other time I'd've asked you to stay,' said Danielle.

'But it was a special occasion,' said Richard.

'Exactly.'

He looked over at the bunch of roses that Nigel had brought home with him; the ones that had replaced Laurence's offering.

'Beautiful flowers too.'

Danielle smiled. She knew exactly what was coming next, and the verbal sparring was beginning to excite her.

'Aren't they?' she agreed.

'Almost as beautiful as the ones you had before.'

She nodded.

'The ones you bought for Nigel.'

'But *you* know I didn't.'

Richard smiled.

'Thank you for not giving the game away,' said Danielle.

'As if I would. I don't believe in interfering between husband and wife.'

I just bet you don't, she thought.

'It was just one of those things,' said Danielle. 'A misunderstanding.'

'Of course. A business acquaintance of your husband's, wasn't it? Or was it?'

'You seem to keep catching me out.'

'I don't mean to. This is the nineties. Anything goes.'

'Does it?' asked Danielle.

'So they tell me.'

Danielle was really enjoying the conversation by now. So much so that she could feel the familiar warmth running down from her belly to between her legs, as her cunt began to lubricate itself.

'I'm afraid I don't know about that,' she said.

'Are you sure?'

'I don't know what you're suggesting.'

Richard put down his cup neatly on its saucer.

'I'm suggesting that you're a naughty girl.'

'Who me?' said Danielle in mock surprise.

'Yes, you.'

'And why do you say that?'

Richard looked towards the fireplace.

'I suggest that, because anyone who leaves her undies in the waste-paper bin must be naughty.'

Danielle suddenly remembered what she had done with her panties on Saturday night before she went to bed and blushed.

Richard saw the blush and smiled.

'Now you know what I mean, don't you?'

'How did you find them?'

'They were hanging over the edge when I came in. You haven't cleaned up properly in here have you?'

Danielle shook her head, got up and went to the bin. It was empty.

'What have you done with them,' she said.

Richard pulled her tiny, torn, black lace panties from the pocket of his trousers and held them up. Even from where she was standing Danielle could see the white stains of her juice in the crotch and blushed again, deeper this time. She felt her cunt hot and wet inside her tight underpants.

'Give them to me,' she demanded.

He put them to his face and breathed in deeply.

'They smell wonderful,' he said. 'Just like I thought you would.'

'You shouldn't say things like that. Now give them back before I get cross.'

'Come and get them,' he said.

'Richard, you're awful.'

He patted the cushion of the sofa next to him with his free hand and said, 'If you want them so badly, come and sit here and ask me nicely.'

'I'll do no such thing.'

'Then I'll keep them for a souvenir.'

'You can't.'

'Why not?'

'Suppose Nigel found out.'

'Then we shan't tell him.'

'But he might find out anyway.'

'Then come and ask me nicely and I'll give them back to you.'

'You promise you won't do anything.'

'Of course.'

Danielle went over and sat next to him and said, 'Give them to me then.'

'I told you, you've got to ask me nicely.'

'I am asking you nicely.'

'Say: Richard, please give me back my panties.'

She sighed. 'Richard, please give me back my panties.'

'Say: Richard, please give me back my black lace panties.'

She did as he said.

'Say: Richard please give me back my black lace panties that are all stained with dried come.'

'No.'

'Say it, or I'll keep them.'

Blushing even redder, if that were possible, she did so.

'Danielle, I believe you're enjoying this,' he said. 'Now say: Richard, please give me back my black lace panties that are all stained with dried come, and were ripped off me before I was fucked.'

'No,' she said. But her cunt was dribbling into her knickers and her breasts felt heavy in her bra and the nipples were so hard, they were beginning to hurt.

'Say it,' he ordered.

'No. Give them to me now.'

'Say it.'

'All right. Richard, please give me my black lace panties that are all stained with dried come, and were ripped off me before I was fucked.'

He smiled in triumph, handed them to her, then caught her wrist, pulled her close and kissed her.

At first she fought back, tugging her wrist out of his grasp and pushing him away with her hands. But as his mouth attached to hers, the desire she felt in her belly blossomed through her body, and as he persevered with the kiss, she softened in his embrace, returning it wholeheartedly.

Meanwhile, back at his office, Nigel was still thinking about his wife and the more he thought of her, the hornier he became. He looked at the calendar on his desk. He had an appointment for lunch with a colleague, then his afternoon was relatively free. He buzzed through to his secretary.

'Cancel lunch,' he said. 'Tell John I was called away suddenly. And if anyone wants me this afternoon, I'm not available. I'll see you in the morning.'

He cleared the small amount of work on his desk and then, whistling cheerfully, he went down to the car park to collect his BMW.

Richard and Danielle wrestled together on the sofa, their kisses hot and horny. Richard pulled down the zip at the front of her shell suit, exposing her breasts – hard and swollen, encased in the tightness of her white bra.

He cupped one in his hand and leant down and kissed the swell of it above the top of her underwear. Danielle pushed his face down into her flesh, and he bit and nibbled at it until she cried out.

The zip on her suit went right down to the crotch and Richard tore it down, until he could see the golden fluff above the elasticated top of her white, hipster briefs. He pushed the suit off her shoulders and down to her waist, then unfastened her bra at the back and tugged it off to unfetter the fullness of her beautiful, pert bosoms.

Her nipples were so swollen with desire they resembled ripe red strawberries and one by one he took them in his mouth and wet their dryness with his spit. Danielle lay back under his ministrations and when he came up for air she tugged his fine woollen sweater over his head. His body was hard and brown and she attached her mouth to his nipples one by one, as he had done to her.

After a few minutes, he reached down and tugged off her trainers and socks. Then he pulled the suit off her legs and dropped it onto the carpet. Standing up, he undid his tight white trousers, pushed them down to his feet, tugged off the casual shoes he was wearing, and pulled off his socks too.

They sat on the sofa again, both dressed only in white underpants and embraced, rubbing their almost naked bodies together and kissing each other's faces and necks.

'Upstairs,' said Richard. 'I want you in bed.'

As one they rose from the sofa and, hand in hand, they left the living room, and side by side walked upstairs to Danielle's marriage bed.

Once inside the bedroom, she drew the curtains slightly and turned to face Richard. She admired his muscular chest and legs, her eyes paying special attention to the large bulge between his legs that strained at the white cotton of his Y-fronts. In his turn he drank in Danielle's shape with his eyes. She looked beautiful in the half light of the room. He'd spent many hours in his lonely house fantasising about what she'd look like naked, and he wasn't in the least disappointed. Her thick blonde hair hung down past her shoulders and caressed the top of her almost-too-perfect white breasts, topped by the hard pinkness of her nipples set in the circles of the aureoles. Her narrow waist swelled into hips that were wide and welcoming, then tapered to legs so long they appeared to go on forever. He looked at her crotch and loved the way that the triangle of material that formed the front of her tiny white panties stretched tightly across her mound of venus.

'You're gorgeous,' he breathed.

'You're not too bad yourself,' she said, and they linked

fingers, gazing into each other's eyes as they moved over towards the bed.

Danielle flipped back the covers and they lay down side by side.

'What time will Nigel be home?' asked Richard.

'Six. Maybe later,' said Danielle. 'We've got hours yet.'

Nigel drove his car into the street where he lived, looking forward to giving his wife a pleasant surprise by coming home early for once.

He felt desire for her building up in his loins and hoped that they would end up in bed for an afternoon of love, sharing one of the cold bottles of white wine that were waiting in the fridge.

He saw that her car was blocking the drive and parked in the street outside, got out of the car, locked it up and walked up the path to the front door. Quietly he let himself in, gently closed the door and went straight to the living room where he could hear the television set playing.

Danielle and Richard literally threw themselves into each other's arms. They lay on the clean white sheets of the bed, pushing their bodies together. Danielle moved so that the lump between his legs fitted into her groin and she moaned as she felt his wedding tackle – still bound by the material of his underwear – shape itself to her.

Their kisses were long and passionate and they ran their hands over each others chests, he tweaking her nipples until they almost sang, and she doing likewise.

Then she felt his fingers under the elastic of her panties and he pushed them down over her thighs towards her feet, so that she could kick them across the room. Then she watched as he tugged down his own underpants and tossed them in the same direction, exposing as magnificent a set of male organs as she had ever seen.

His prong was long, thick, and red, with an enormous knob at the end. Poking out of his dark pubic hair and behind his cock lay his big hard balls. She put down her hand to touch them, and she felt the fullness of the sacs between his legs.

'Has it been a long time?' she asked.

'Too long.'

'Have patience my sweet. It won't be long now before you can empty them into me.'

Nigel walked into the living room to find it empty except for the TV in the corner burbling merrily away to itself. He stopped in the doorway and looked at the clothes scattered everywhere. His wife's shell-suit, bra, white socks and trainers were scattered haphazardly across the furniture and carpet, entwined with a pair of men's white trousers, a yellow sweater that looked vaguely familiar, two pale yellow socks and a pair of white casual shoes. He picked one up. Men's, size nine.

He could hardly believe his eyes and was so shocked he had to put one hand on the back of the sofa for support. Then he noticed two cups and saucers and two plates on the floor and finally, lying between the cushions of the sofa, the torn and stained black knickers that Danielle had been wearing before their night of love the previous Saturday.

Nigel turned and very quietly left the room and looked upstairs. From above he could faintly hear the sound of voices. One male, one female. He knew them both. He was about to call out, but contained himself and crept up the carpeted stairs to the first floor of the house.

Danielle and Richard could not get enough of each other's bodies. They wanted to kiss and touch every inch of each other, and explore every orifice with their tongues and fingers.

They slid around the bed together, licking and sucking as they went. Danielle could feel Richard's cock banging against her, and Richard loved the way her wet cunt slid along his skin as she climbed over him in search of somewhere new to explore.

Eventually they ended up lying side by side, Richard's head pointing in the direction of the top of the bed, and Danielle's pointing towards the foot, with her blonde mane spread across his groin, and his cock in her mouth, and his face between her legs, lapping at the open slit of her pussy in the *soixante neuf* position.

And that was how Nigel saw them as he silently reached the top of the stairs and looked into his and Danielle's bedroom. He could hardly believe his eyes. There was his beautiful young wife clearly to be seen, licking the long fat member of a neighbour – someone Nigel had always thought of as a friend – whilst the neighbour's head was buried deeply into her delectable and fragrant cunt.

His wife and another man! Having an adulterous sexual encounter. In Nigel's own house. In the very bed that he and Danielle had only shared the night before. And he'd never suspected a thing.

Suddenly Nigel realised what had brought on his wife's sudden reawakening of sexual interest. She had a lover.

Maybe more than one. His head spun at the thought.

Nigel stood transfixed by the sight and sounds of the couple's lovemaking. He watched them writhing together in ecstasy, and heard the slurping noises their mouths made on each other's sexual parts.

He knew that he should be angry. That he should barge in on their romp, and catch them *in flagrante delicto*. He knew that he should drag Richard off his wife's body and beat him to within an inch of his life and throw him naked out into the street, then return and give Danielle a sound thrashing for her sins. But instead, he found himself enjoying the sight. He'd never seen anyone making love before, except on the videos that he'd seen in various hotel rooms with blue channels on the television sets. Videos that he'd watched on one of the many lonely nights he'd spent away from home on business. But this was real flesh. Real sweat, real passion. And it was his wife that he was watching. The woman who had promised to be faithful until death parted them, when they'd taken their marriage vows together just a few short years before.

And he could smell the sex, smell it strongly in the warm air of his house. The sweet sharpness of it filled his nostrils, until it made him feel dizzy with lust and his prick begin to swell between his legs.

So, instead of confronting them, he stayed where he was. Motionless, in the darkness at the head of the stairs, where he knew they couldn't see him, even if they had bothered to look. Nigel knew they weren't going to though, so involved in giving each other pleasure were they.

He saw them pull away from each other's genitals, and Danielle slid round, so that she could kiss Richard's mouth again, tasting her own juice on his lips. He saw Richard's hand go down to the triangle of blonde hair between Danielle's legs, and she opened them so that his fingers could slip with a squelching noise into her open quim. As he frigged her, Danielle took Richard's cock into her hand and gently wanked it, until it seemed to grow another inch in length and the same in circumference. And then, without a word passing between them, Nigel knew they were ready for the final part of the act. Danielle lay back with her legs wide apart, as Richard mounted her body, and she steered his pork sword between the delectable lips of her cunt with her fingers. She accepted the whole length of it in one swift, sure movement, until they became one, and began to move in the age old motion of love.

Nigel could hear them whispering then, but could only make out the occasional word: 'darling', 'sweetheart', 'lover'. Each syllable was like a painful arrow through his heart, but each arrow seemed to make his cock grow harder in his trousers.

As the tempo of their love increased, he heard Danielle beginning to moan in a way that he thought she had only before moaned for her husband.

'Harder,' she called out. 'Fuck me harder. I want you. I want your spunk. I need it inside me.'

And the more she cried out for his sex, the harder Richard shafted her.

As the fuck grew more frenzied and the volume of their voices became louder, Nigel could clearly hear every word they spoke.

'I want you too, darling,' cried Richard. 'I want to fill you with my seed.'

'Then do it. I want it too. I want your juice inside me. I want it to burn me.'

Nigel could see Richard's hard, hairy balls bouncing up and down on Danielle's arse as he screwed her and his buttocks were tense as he slammed himself into her body.

Nigel's hand went to his fly and he unzipped himself, taking his cock in his hand. It was hard and hot and he began to wank himself in time to his wife and her lover's movements.

The bed banged against the wall as their lovemaking grew even more intense, and Nigel felt himself ready to come, but didn't dare. He wanted to leave no evidence that he had been in the house. Instead, he stopped reluctantly and pushed his cock back into his trousers, as with mutual cries of pleasure his wife and his neighbour climaxed together.

Nigel looked on in amazement, as he literally saw Richard's balls empty themselves into Danielle's willing pussy.

As the two lovers collapsed together onto the bed, Nigel quietly turned and went downstairs, fastening his trousers on the way. Then he let himself out of the house, closing the door silently behind him, and crept down the path back to his car.

'What was that noise?' said Danielle as she and Richard lay in a sweaty embrace together.

'I didn't hear anything.'

She tensed. 'I thought it was . . . No, it couldn't have been. I'm imagining things.' Then she turned to her new conquest. 'Was that good, Richard?' she asked.

'Wonderful, my love.'

She kissed him hard on the lips, as she felt his jism running out of her cunt, down the crack of her bottom and onto the clean sheets of her bed.

'Yes it was rather, wasn't it?' she said.

24

Nigel drove back to his office and when he walked in, his secretary said, 'I didn't think you'd be back this afternoon.'

'Change of plans,' he said, and went into his office, sat behind his desk and swivelled his chair so that he could look out of the window.

He sat there for more than an hour, thinking about what he had witnessed at home. He ran the film of his wife making love to another man through his mind over and over again. He couldn't seem to get the images out of his brain. He knew he should be furious, but somehow, the more he thought about it, the more aroused he became, until the desire he felt for Danielle was like a fierce pain in his balls.

Eventually he picked up the phone and dialled his home number. Danielle answered on the third ring. 'It's me,' he said.

'Hello, darling,' replied his wife, and he could hear no trace in her voice of what he knew she'd been doing not two hours before. 'How are you?'

'Fine,' he said. 'Just thought I'd give you a ring.'

'That's nice.'

'Had a good day?'

'Just the usual.'

He could almost imagine from listening to her, that she was telling the truth. Maybe, he thought, what she was doing with Richard that afternoon *was* the usual.

'What time will you be home?' she asked.

'Six. Maybe a little after.'

'Fine. Dinner will be ready.'

'Good. I've been thinking about you today.'

'I've been thinking about you too,' said Danielle.

'Good. Then I'll see you at six. Love you.'

'Love you too.' They made their farewells and hung up.

Danielle put down the phone and sat back on the sofa where she'd been sitting when Nigel rang, thinking about what had happened earlier in the day.

After their first bout of passionate sex, she and Richard had laid together in bed half asleep, stroking and kissing and nibbling each other, whispering about how marvellous their lovemaking had been.

'Who was that who brought you the roses?' asked Richard after a while.

Danielle smiled. She had wondered how long it would be before he asked.

'My lover,' she replied cooly.

'Where did you meet him?'

'At a hotel.'

'What happened?'

Danielle smiled again, and told him, not leaving out any details. As she spoke she felt Richard's manhood begin to grow again, and poke into the flesh of her thigh. Between the words she was speaking, he began to kiss her more passionately until only the kisses seemed to matter and the story was forgotten.

She stroked Richard's knob until it was fully erect again and they made love once more, this time doggy fashion with Danielle kneeling on the bed in front of him as he slid into her pussy from behind. As he fucked her, he reached round and began to play with her clitoris until she came repeatedly. Only after she had had four or five orgasms in fewer minutes, did he pump at her harder until he ejected a stream of hot semen into her womb.

They collapsed onto the bed together again and lay in a sweaty heap.

After a few minutes Danielle said, 'Richard, you'd better go. I've got things to do.'

'Like?'

'Like clean the place up and get Nigel's dinner ready. A woman's work is never done, you know.'

'I hope your work on me's not finished, that's for sure.'

'For today it is. Don't be greedy.'

'I'm greedy for you,' he said, and began to caress her breasts again.

'Stop it,' she said firmly, rolled over, got off the bed, found her knickers and stepped into them. 'Now get dressed and go.'

'Can I come again?'

'Isn't twice in one afternoon enough?'

'You know what I mean.'

'We'll see,' she said, and picked his underpants up off the floor and threw them at him.

Reluctantly he pulled them on and they went downstairs and put on the rest of their clothes.

'When can I see you again?' asked Richard.

'I'll call you. I've got your number.'

Even more reluctantly he allowed Danielle to usher him

out of the house. 'And next time,' she said, 'come in the back way.'

25

When Nigel arrived home at ten past six, his wife was in the kitchen, putting the finishing touches to dinner.

She was wearing the same shell-suit he had last seen on the floor of his living room that afternoon, tangled up with Richard's yellow sweater.

When Nigel saw her standing by the stove – one hip cocked against the wall – the ache in his balls flared up again, and he felt his prick swell with desire.

I wonder if she's wearing the same undies? he thought. All wet and filthy with spunk. And as he did so his cock grew even more.

Danielle stopped what she was doing and came over and kissed her husband. 'Hello, darling,' she said. 'Had a good day?'

'An interesting one,' he replied.

'That's nice. Dinner will be ready soon. Do you want to open some wine.'

Right then, all Nigel wanted to open were his wife's legs, but he buried the desire and went to the fridge.

When he'd done the chore he said, 'I'll just pop upstairs and change. Won't be a minute.'

He went upstairs to the bedroom, which was as clean and tidy as it always was, and once again he could almost imagine he'd dreamt what he'd seen happening there that afternoon.

He went straight to the neatly made bed and pulled back the covers. The sheets were fresh from the laundry. He smiled to himself and went over to the washing hamper.

Buried under a couple of soiled shirts were a pair of white sheets. He pulled them out and unfolded them. One was badly stained with the evidence of sex. In the middle of the sheet were several damp grey stains. He put his nose to them and sniffed. He could clearly smell the same bittersweet tang as he'd smelt in the air whilst he'd watched Danielle and Richard rolling all over the bed, a few hours before.

He smiled again, and refolded the sheets. Before he put them back, he went through the hamper looking for any of Danielle's underwear that contained the same tell-tale stains. There were none.

That was when he was sure she was still wearing the same knickers she had worn all day.

And that was when he was sure he was going to strip them off her and lick the gusset clean.

He smiled again, returned the washing to the hamper as it had been, and changed into jeans and a polo shirt.

When he got back downstairs Danielle was dishing out the food.

After Richard had left, she'd gone upstairs and changed the bed linen. She knew that she should have a shower and put on clean clothes, but she didn't want to lose the delightful sensation she was feeling in her cunt in the aftermath of her multiple orgasms, which was exacerbated by the mixture of hers and Richard's juices dribbling out of her slit and soaking her knickers each time she moved.

I'll change later, she thought, but kept putting it off until she heard Nigel's key in the door, and she knew it was too late.

She mentally shrugged. So what? she thought. It'll make dinner all the more enjoyable if I'm sitting in a puddle of come.

And indeed it did.

After dinner was over, the wine almost finished and the dishes piled up in the dishwasher, Danielle said from the doorway of the living room, 'I think I'll go and take a shower.'

'Don't go,' said Nigel, who was sitting on the sofa. 'Stay and talk.'

'If you like,' said Danielle. 'What shall we talk about?'

'I don't know. Come and sit by me.'

Danielle joined Nigel on the sofa. He put his arm around her and pulled her close.

'I thought you wanted to talk,' she said.

'I do. I think we should have a dinner party.'

'What a good idea,' said Danielle. 'It's been ages. Who shall we invite?'

'How about some of the neighbours?'

'If you like. Who?'

'I thought we'd ask Richard from over the road.'

He felt Danielle stiffen in his embrace.

'Who else?'

'Has he got a girlfriend?'

'I don't know.'

Suddenly Danielle wondered if Nigel knew what had happened that afternoon. It would explain the noise she'd heard after she and Richard had finished fucking and the unusual fact that Nigel had rung in the middle of the day.

Surely not, she thought. Am I just being paranoid?

'What if he hasn't?' she asked.

'Then just ask him. A nice quiet dinner party for the three of us. Wouldn't you like that?'

'If you would.'

'Yes, I would. Why don't you go over and ask him tomorrow. Saturday would be a good day for us, wouldn't it?'

'All right,' said Danielle. 'I think I'll take that shower now.'

Nigel kissed her. 'Why don't you let me make you dirty before you do.'

Danielle felt a thrill of excitement in her belly. Does he know? She thought again. And if he doesn't, will he guess from the smell of sex in my cunt? He hadn't the last time, in Southampton after her quickie with the waiter in the broom cupboard. Or had he? Her mind was in turmoil as the second male hand of the day pulled down the zip at the front of her shell-suit.

'Nigel!' she said. 'What's come over you lately?'

'Just trying to put the magic back into our marriage, darling,' he said. 'Remember?'

26

Nigel pushed the top of the shell suit off Danielle's shoulders, just had Richard had done earlier, to reveal the same white bra. Nigel's head went between her breasts, once again, the same as Richard's had done.

Christ, thought Danielle, looking over her husband's head. Just give a man a pair of tits and he'll play for hours.

She felt his tongue lapping at her cleavage and the earlier thrill of excitement began to grow.

And I'm just as bad, she thought. I'm beginning to go cock-simple.

Nigel could smell sweat on his wife's body and he knew that when he got between her legs he'd smell and taste the detritus of her afternoon sex, and the thought almost drove him crazy.

Once again he was torn between jealousy and desire, but once again desire won and his cock was swollen with the blood of need for sexual release.

He pulled the suit down to her feet, knelt between Danielle's legs and ripped her panties down to her ankles. He could clearly see the dark stains in the crotch of the white knickers and as her cunt was revealed he smelt for the third time that day the stink of sex emanating from her body. The smell almost made him drunk and he roughly pushed her legs apart. Her pubic hair was dark and matted with gunk and he stuck his face into the dampness of it as if he wanted to drown in her liquids.

Danielle's pussy was sore from her earlier fuck, but she didn't care. The violence of Nigel's attack on her womanhood was the biggest turn-on she'd felt since she'd been fucked by Dave and Johnny Harvey in the caravan at the their garage in Drenham. She kicked at the clothes that constrained her ankles and pushed her suit and knickers off over her shoes so that she could open her legs wider and allow her husband greater access to her sex.

She slid down on the cushion of the sofa and lifted her legs over his shoulders, until she was bent almost double and her cunt was wide open to his searching tongue.

The lips of his mouth and the lips of her cunt slid over each other in a frenzy as he slurped and sucked at her. He chewed on her clitoris until she thought he was going to bite it off, but the feeling only made her more excited. He was drinking Richard's come out of her and she loved it.

She grabbed his hair and tugged his head off her. 'Kiss me,' she demanded. 'I want to taste it.'

He almost jumped up her body to get to her face and soon they were enjoying long, open mouthed snogging. His mouth stank of her sex and she licked the taste off his lips, as if it was the dregs of a fine vintage wine.

As they kissed, Nigel tore off his clothes. As soon as his cock was revealed, harder and more swollen than Danielle could ever remember seeing it, she grabbed at it like a drowning man reaching for a lifebelt.

The gland felt massive in her hands and she massaged even more blood into it, until it felt as hard and stiff as a poker.

Lying back on the sofa she manoeuvred the hot length of it into her quim and pulled his buttocks close to her so that she could get the complete sensation of being filled with living flesh.

Nigel's arse bucked under her hands as he slammed himself into her, then pulled back, only to crash himself even harder into the soft centre of her womanhood.

She responded with all the strength she could muster, matching his strokes, and feeling the length of him rubbing the wetness of her love tunnel.

His cock felt enormous, like a huge battering ram trying to break her in two.

Danielle loved every second of the fierce fuck as the perspiration poured off Nigel and dripped onto her body, mixed with her own sweat and rolled off to wet the material of the sofa covers.

The excitement in her belly grew as his strokes became shorter and harder. The sweat flew from their bodies, and he drove himself into her harder and harder until finally, with a long drawn out cry, he shot his load into the welcoming pussy.

His spunk burnt her insides like liquid fire and, as with his last thrust he spent all his energy, she matched his orgasm with one of her own.

27

Later, lying in bed with Nigel snoring next to her, Danielle kept thinking about what had happened that evening. She was almost sure that Nigel knew about her dalliance with Richard. She hadn't been married to the man for five years without knowing something about the way his mind worked. But on the other hand she couldn't be certain, and it niggled at her. If he did know, none of this made sense. Why did he want to invite her lover for dinner? She was sure that he didn't want to have a fight with him about it. If he did, he could have done it when he saw the pair of them in bed together.

Maybe he likes the idea, she thought. If he does know, that's all it can be. And the idea excited her tremendously. But Nigel had never expressed the fantasy of her being screwed by another man. Never even brought the subject up. But if it was true that he did know, and he *did* like the idea, it had certainly improved his performance in the sexual stakes. Which was something.

She was still puzzled, but smiling, as she fell asleep ten minutes later.

The next morning Nigel was in an effusive mood as he got ready to go to work. He joined Danielle in the shower and insisted on washing her all over. Then he kept touching her intimately as she prepared his breakfast and, of course, she couldn't help becoming aroused, although he refused to finish her off.

It's as if he wants me ready for sex, she thought, as he slid his hand under her dressing gown and teased her naked breasts for the dozenth time, while she waited for the coffee pot to boil. But not with him.

'Don't forget to ask Richard about Saturday night,' was the last thing that Nigel said before slipping on his jacket and leaving the house, giving Danielle a long, lingering kiss on the mouth as he went.

You're pushing us together, she thought as she waved him off. But if that's what you want, on your own head be it.

She gave the house a perfunctory clean and drove to the supermarket for some bits and pieces of shopping. Then she returned home and got changed, before going over to invite her lover for dinner with her husband and herself. Even though what she was doing was strange, the thought of it, coupled with the intimate caresses that Nigel had given her earlier, had her ready for fucking. As she stepped into a pair of black net panties she could see the beads of moisture already gathering in the hair between her legs and she carefully wiped them away with a tissue.

She caught her breasts up in a matching, strapless, net bra and put on a black silk blouse and a black miniskirt. She slipped her bare feet into black, low-heeled shoes and covered the whole ensemble with her Burberry raincoat.

She left the house and clip-clopped over the road to Richard's front door and rang the bell. As she waited on the doorstep, hands in pockets, she gazed at the blind, curtained windows of the other houses that overlooked his and wondered if any of the neighbours were peering out at her, and if they were, whether they suspected what was happening.

Richard answered the door within a minute. He was unshaven and his hair was wild. He was wearing tight black jeans and a blue denim shirt. His feet were bare and he was holding a slice of toast in one hand.

'Danielle,' he said, pushing the hand that wasn't holding the toast through his hair to tidy it a little. 'What's the matter? This is a surprise.'

She nodded. 'Isn't it?' she said. 'Aren't you going to ask me in?'

'Of course. I'm sorry, but the place is a bit of a mess, I wasn't expecting anyone.'

'More of the joys of bachelorhood,' she commented.

He pulled a face and opened the door wider to allow her access.

She walked into the hall and Richard kissed her on the lips, but she ducked out of his embrace before the kiss got too serious. 'Where to?' she asked. 'And don't you dare say, "to the bedroom".'

'First on the left,' said Richard, and Danielle turned into the living room. It was reasonably tidy, but Richard insisted on rushing round and pushing things into drawers and under the cushions of the three piece suite before saying, 'Give me your coat and sit down. Do you want some coffee?'

'Love some,' said Danielle.

'It's only instant, remember?'

She smiled. 'Instant will do fine. White. No sugar.'

Richard took her coat off her shoulders and admired the

shape of her breasts under the thin material of her shirt. 'What an attractive outfit.' he said.

Danielle posed, with her hand on her hip. 'Do you think so?'

'You knew I would. That's why you chose it.'

Danielle fluttered her eyelashes and Richard vanished in the direction of the kitchen. She walked around the room, picking up and putting down various ornaments before sitting on one of the two armchairs that faced the dead fireplace.

He was back within a few minutes carefully balancing two steaming mugs on a tray. He set them down on the coffee table between the armchairs and sat down opposite Danielle.

'To what do I owe this pleasure?' he asked, once he was comfortable. 'I thought you were going to ring me. Aren't you worried what the neighbours will say?'

'I'm here on a legitimate mission,' she replied. 'With an invitation.'

Richard looked at her quizzically. 'Invitation? For what?'

'For dinner at our house.'

Richard looked amazed. 'Are you joking?'

'Not at all. It was Nigel's idea.'

Richard's face split into a grin. 'My God,' he said. 'Wonders will never cease.'

'That's exactly what I thought. He asked me if you had a girlfriend you could bring along to make up a foursome?'

Richard shook his head. 'Sorry. I don't. I told you that.'

'But I could hardly tell Nigel. He might have asked under what circumstances you told *me*.'

Richard's grin widened. 'And you could hardly say, could you?'

Danielle's grin matched his. 'Hardly,' she agreed. Then she became serious. 'I've got a feeling he knows something, or at least suspects.'

'Why?'

She shrugged. 'Just a feeling,' she said.

'Has he said anything?'

'No.'

'Then maybe he's just being friendly.'

'I don't know . . .'

'Are you being paranoid, Danielle? Does he know about your other lover?'

'Christ, I hope not.'

'There you are then. Paranoia.'

'I certainly hope so. Do you want to come?'

'What, to dinner?'

'Yes, to dinner, you fool.'

'When?'

'Saturday night.'

'Sounds good to me. I told you that I wanted to taste some of your cooking. But seriously, I don't have anyone to bring. That was the truth. I haven't as much as taken a woman out for ages.'

'Yes you have.' said Danielle.

Richard smiled. 'You know what I mean. Does that make a difference?'

'Not according to Nigel. Come on your own.'

'My God, but it's going to be strange. I've never sat down for dinner with someone I've made love to and her husband before.'

'There's always a first time.'

'Isn't there? And talking of that . . .'

'What?'

'Why don't you come and sit over here by me?'

'Are you propositioning me?'

'Come here and find out.'

And Danielle did.

She joined Richard on the sofa and squeezed herself down between his body and the arm of the chair. As she slid down, her skirt rose up her naked thighs and exposed the shape of her mound and the tight bush of blonde hair under her net panties.

'Did you wear those for me?' asked Richard.

'No. The milkman.'

'Do you let him into your bed too?' he said, kissing her mouth.

'Only when there's an 'R' in the month,' she replied saucily.

'So we're all right,' he said, as his hand went to her breast.

'Ever so,' agreed Danielle, as her hand in its turn found the satisfyingly fat bulge that was growing under the denim of his jeans. 'Ever so.'

They kissed again, their tongues entwining, as Richard found the top button of her shirt and undid it, then the next, before sliding his hands under the silk, on to the net of her bra that forced her breasts upwards and apart and made them look so enticing under the fine material of the garment. 'I love your tits,' he said. 'They're so beautiful.'

'Most men do,' replied Danielle. 'I don't know what they see in them.'

Richard put his head down and kissed the skin of her neck, then slid his tongue over the rise of her breasts. 'If you give me a year, I might be able to tell you.'

'That good, eh?' said Danielle.

'Better.'

'I'll take your word for it.'

As they spoke she was rubbing his cock through the material of his jeans, scratching at it with her fingernails.

'God, that feels great,' said Richard.

'Get it out for me, I want to lick it.'

Richard undid the buttons at his flies and wrestled his knob out. Danielle bent over and attached her lips to the glans. She sucked in a mouthful of hot flesh and ran her tongue round the top of it, in and out of the hole, tasting the soft skin inside.

She sucked and licked the hard flesh, gobbling at the end with lascivious satisfaction, and almost devouring the length of the tool as she slid the knob along the back of her throat.

Richard loved the attention she was giving his tool, and never wanted it to stop. But her rude mouth wanted its own satisfaction, and within a minute or two he felt the sweet pain of a coming ejaculation, and pushed her head down on his cock as he spunked his load into her mouth.

'You bitch,' he said, when he was finished. 'I was enjoying that.'

Danielle swallowed the last of his jism and licked her lips for any stray drops that she might have missed.

When she had finished, she said. 'Let's go to bed. That's made me really horny, and I want your cock up me.'

Richard's bedroom was as tidy as the living room had been, except that the large double bed had not been made. Together they dived onto it, kissing passionately, and Richard's knob was already hard again as Danielle went down on him for the second time that morning. The skin of it was sweet and damp with her scent, and she licked the length of it, and sucked the hair around his balls, rolling him over so that she could lick the crack of his arse and stick her tongue into his hairy anus. When her tongue entered the hole, he pushed his groin deep into the mattress with delight.

She pulled her head back and said, 'Don't you dare come. I want your spunk in me.'

'I won't,' he said into the pillow, 'but you're driving me crazy, doing that.'

Danielle's cunt was so wet it felt like a river was running down between her legs.

'Then get inside me,' she cried. 'Let me have your cock in my cunt.'

Richard rolled over again, threw her down onto the mattress, and crawled on top of her. She felt his knob push open the lips of her pussy and slide into the beautiful wetness there. He began to screw her. She writhed underneath him, and he lay his whole weight on her to keep her still. She pushed her hips up to meet his, and they soon found their rhythm and fucked each other until a scream ripped from her throat as she squeezed out a come onto his beautiful weapon. 'More,' she shouted. 'More cock,' and with a beatific smile, Richard pounded at her, until he loosed his sperm into his lover's body.

28

Totally shattered after their sex, Danielle and Richard lay together in the wreck of his bed, the skin of their bodies messy and gooey from their own and each other's sweat and come, so that they stuck together where they touched. Danielle tugged the duvet over them and snuggled up into Richard's arms. 'We stink,' she said.

'I like it,' he replied.

'So do I. Just think, I wasn't at all keen on you until the other day.'

'Weren't you?'

'No. I thought you were a dreadful letch.'

'I was. Over you. I couldn't help it. But I didn't think you'd noticed.'

'I noticed all right. And then you tried to blackmail me.'

'I wouldn't have really. I was just trying it on. I was terribly jealous of the bloke who brought you those flowers.'

'Are you still?'

'Yes. And of Nigel, and of anyone else who's ever had you.'

'That's sweet.'

'So, are you keen on me now?'

'Yes. I suppose I am a little.'

'Just a little?'

'For the time being.'

'And I have to make do with that?'

'I'm a married woman. You shouldn't say things like that to married women.'

'And if you weren't married?'

'That would be different.'

'That's good. Do you see him regularly?'

'Who?'

'The bloke who brought you the roses.'

'Sometimes.'

'Will you see him again?'

'If I want to.'

'Even though you're seeing me?'

'That won't last forever.'

'How do you know?'

'I just do. But don't think about it, I'm with you now, aren't I?'

'Yes you are, aren't you?' And his fingers went down to her pussy again. 'Sore?' he asked.

'A little. Your cock's very big and hard.'

'I bet you say that to all the boys.'

'I do not.'

'Just to me?'

And anyone else with a big hard cock, thought Danielle, mischievously.

'That's right,' she said.

'I always think you're taking the mickey.'

'Sometimes I am,' she replied. And sometimes she was. 'But not always,' she said. 'Anyway, I think I'll go home now. Are you still coming to dinner on Saturday?'

'Try and keep me away. What time shall I come round?'

'I'll phone you and let you know.'

'You can't. I've got to go away tonight on business, and I won't be back until Saturday. It's a good thing you caught me this morning.'

'Is that right?' said Danielle, reaching down for his cock. 'And I did catch you, didn't I?'

'You can say that again.'

'Shall we have one more before I go?'

'You're insatiable, Danielle,' he said unbelievingly. 'I don't know if I can manage it.'

She felt his penis thickening under her caress. 'Oh, I don't know, Richard,' she said. 'I think you're more capable than you think.'

'My God,' he said. 'You have a hell of an effect on me.'

Danielle climbed on top of him and manipulated his prick up into her crack, slid down the length of it, and began to gently bounce up and down and move slowly from side to side, working the muscles of her vagina onto Richard's love pump as she went.

'It seems like a crime to waste it,' she said breathlessly, as her clitoris was massaged by his rod. 'A hell of a waste.' And she contracted hard on his prick, and drew his semen up into her, before flopping down on top of him with a cry of satisfaction.

They lay together for another half an hour before Danielle said, 'I'd better be going, and let you get ready for your trip. Otherwise I'll be here all day.'

'I wouldn't mind,' said Richard.

'You're lovely,' she replied, and kissed him on his stubbly cheeks and got out of bed. She went to the bathroom and got dressed again. 'You're going to need clean sheets, darling,' she said as she went.

When she went back into the bedroom Richard was still lying in the wreck of the bed where she'd left him. 'Have I exhausted you?' she asked.

'Pretty well.'

'Are you going to miss me when you're away?'

'Every minute. Will you miss me?'

She smiled down at him and said, 'We'll have to see. Come round about seven-thirty on Saturday. I'll cook something special for you.' And she blew him a kiss, went downstairs, put on her mac again and went home.

29

The rest of the week passed quietly enough. Nigel was delighted to learn that Richard had accepted the invitation to dinner on Saturday night. Far more delighted than Danielle thought was necessary, which only confirmed her suspicions that he knew about her infidelity, which meant that he had some deeper motive than just a cosy dinner *à trois* for wanting the three of them together. Possibly a *menage à trois*, she concluded, which suited her just fine.

As far as sex was concerned between Danielle and her husband during those few days, there was a lot of foreplay but no consummation, and she was more convinced than ever that he knew about her and Richard.

By Saturday morning, all the caresses and teasing that she had received from Nigel had left Danielle hot and horny, which was just what he wanted. He had his own plans for Saturday night. And they were precisely what Danielle thought they were.

The fact that Richard was away frustrated her even more. If he'd been around, at least she could have used his cock to satisfy herself. She even tried phoning Laurence, but his answer phone seemed to be permanently switched on.

She spent all of Saturday afternoon preparing a sumptuous meal. She made a salmon mousse to start, a fillet mignon for the entrée, and pears poached in wine for dessert. At five o'clock, when the food was all but ready, she went upstairs to prepare for the evening. She had a long soak in the bath, then washed and dried her hair. She took particular care with her make-up, trying to make herself look as attractive as possible. She knew she couldn't go another night without a fuck, and quite frankly she didn't care which of the two men she had cooked for gave it to her. Hopefully, it would be both of them.

If that's what you want, Nigel, she thought, as she caressed herself between her legs under the warm, perfumed water of her bath, then that's exactly what you'll get.

She dressed in black silk French knickers over a black G-string which bit into the tender skin of her cunt and made her lubricate from the moment she put it on. She wore no bra, just a silk camisole that matched the French knickers and came down to her waist. The feel of the silk on her breasts immediately aroused them. She chose a pair of sheer, seamed nylons and a black suspender belt to hold them up. On top she wore a high-necked black silk dress that was so tight her hardened nipples were clearly visible through the material. On her feet she wore very high-heeled, black patent leather shoes.

If this doesn't get the boys going, she thought, as she did a twirl in front of the bedroom mirror, then nothing will.

When she went downstairs, Nigel – dressed in black trousers, and a maroon waistcoat, unbuttoned over a crisp white shirt – was preparing a jug of martini cocktails. He whistled as she walked into the living room.

'You look stunning, Danielle,' he said. 'Absolutely stunning.'

'Thank you, darling,' she replied. 'Are the drinks ready?'

'Of course,' and he poured her one of the freezing, lethal cocktails.

At seven-thirty precisely the doorbell rang, and Nigel answered it. Richard came in wearing a navy blue suit, cream shirt and a wildly patterned tie, carrying an off-licence carrier bag that clinked as he walked. When he saw her, he stopped in the living room doorway. 'Good evening, Danielle,' he said. 'Can I compliment you on your outfit? You look like a million dollars.'

'Thank you,' said Danielle for the second time that evening. 'Would you like a martini?'

'My favourite cocktail,' said Richard. 'I'd love one.'

Danielle filled a glass for him and he took an appreciative swig. 'Just how I like them,' he said. 'Very strong.'

'That's just how I make them,' said Nigel. 'Do sit down old chap, whilst I put this wine in the fridge.'

When Nigel had left the room, Danielle said. 'I'm sure he knows about us, Richard. He's been in a *very* strange mood all week.'

Richard shrugged. 'Well he doesn't seem very upset. Just the opposite.'

'I know,' said Danielle. 'It's all very odd.'

When Nigel came back, they showed Richard into the dining room, where the table was set for three, and Danielle and Nigel fetched the first course from the kitchen, together with the hostess trolley where the fillet, potatoes and vegetables were keeping hot. Nigel poured the wine and they served themselves and began to eat.

The meal was a great success and when they had finished all three courses, three bottles of wine, and the coffee was bubbling away in its pot, the two men were full of praise for Danielle's culinary skills. Modestly she accepted their compliments and Nigel opened the brandy bottle.

When they'd drunk their coffee and a couple of large brandies each, he suggested taking the liqueur into the living room where it was more comfortable.

Danielle and Richard readily agreed and, rather tipsily, the three of them left the washing-up, and trooped into the other room.

Richard and Nigel sat together on the sofa and Danielle took the armchair opposite.

'This is very pleasant,' said Nigel. 'Shall we have some music?'

The other two concurred, and he stood up and went over to the stereo and chose a CD by Womack & Womack.

'Do you want to dance?' he said to Danielle as the first slow, sexy soul track oozed out of the speakers.

'Sure,' she replied, and levered herself out of her chair.

She went into his arms and felt the ridge of his erection through his trousers, and her pussy that had been leaking juices into her knickers all evening began to lubricate again.

She rubbed herself up against him as they began to dance, and he pushed back in response.

As the song continued, they stood, hips together and dry humped each other, completely oblivious of the third party present.

When the song ended, Nigel said in a choked voice, 'Why don't you dance with Richard now? Richard, would you like that?'

'I'd be delighted,' said the other man, who had been a silent witness to Danielle and Nigel's zipless fuck. He stood up and took her out of her husband's arms as the second song began, which was as slow and sensual as the first.

Danielle fitted into his embrace and pushed up against his groin too, and was delighted to feel another erection pushing into her soft flesh.

As the music filled the room and her ears, she leant her head against Richard's shoulder and allowed him to lead her in an erotic dance in front of her husband.

When the music ended, they stood pressed together, until the third song on the album started, and once again they moved together in a slow dance of sex. Danielle was loving every moment. She had two men in the palm of her hand and she knew that before long she would have both their cocks there too, before allowing them entry into the most private parts of her body. She allowed the music to drift past her and Richard to guide her through another erotic dance which made her more horny by the moment. When the song ended, Richard led her back by her hand to her seat.

'Another drink?' asked Nigel.

Although her head was already spinning, Danielle nodded assent and he poured a large slug of brandy into her glass.

She sat back down in her seat and crossed her legs, knowing that both the men were looking up her skirt at her stocking tops. Although she was getting drunk, she felt sufficiently in control of the situation not to care.

Nigel and Richard once again sat opposite Danielle, drinks in hand, and Nigel said, 'Do you think I've got a beautiful wife, Richard?'

'Sensational,' replied Richard.

'I agree entirely. And a good cook too.'

'Certainly.'

'Everything a man could want in a woman.'

'Without doubt.'

Danielle was bathing in the compliments that they were giving her, and she knew exactly in which direction it was leading, and she felt more of a thrill with every word they said.

'Come and sit between us,' Nigel said to his wife. 'I'm sure you'll be more comfortable over here.'

Danielle did as he suggested. She got rather unsteadily to her feet and walked over to the sofa and sat between her husband and her lover.

As she say down, Nigel kissed her on the cheek, slid his arm over her shoulder and said drunkenly, 'I love you Danielle.'

'And I love you too,' she replied.

He put his hand in her lap and she felt it brush over her mound of venus, and she opened her legs slightly at his touch. He ran his fingers up the bodice of her dress and over her breasts which only made her nipples harder and protrude further through the silk.

'What *are* you doing?' said Danielle.

'Don't you like it?'

'I didn't say that.'

He covered one breast with his hand and felt the hard nub of gristle on top of the soft, pliable flesh, and she moaned softly at his touch. 'I can tell,' he said.

Danielle wriggled under his caress, and glanced over at Richard sitting on the other side of her. He was looking at Nigel's hand, and she saw him lick his lips. She reached over and took his hand and placed it on her other breast.

'Don't be selfish, Nigel,' she said. 'Remember that we have a guest.'

Nigel grinned wolfishly. 'Sorry Richard,' he said. 'I was quite forgetting myself.'

Danielle lay back and opened her legs even further as the two men gently massaged her breasts through her clothing. Her belly was burning with desire and she desperately wanted to feel their hands on her bare skin.

Nigel leaned his head close to hers and kissed her on her mouth, and she responded hungrily, sucking his lips and tongue into it, and forcing her own tongue onto his.

His hand pressed her breast harder and she pushed her torso up against his and Richard's fingers.

As she felt their strong hands on her, she opened her legs even further and felt her skirt slide up her legs to expose her naked thighs above her stocking tops. Nigel's other hand moved down between them and slowly worked its way up to find the edge of lace on the legs of her French knickers, and the G-string beneath it. She knew she was soaking and the feel of his hand on her cunt made her want a cock inside it even more.

She grabbed Richard's hand and forced it down between her legs to join her husband's, and they both played with the entrance to her pussy until she though she'd scream with need and desire.

She could see their erections clearly through their trousers and she touched them both simultaneously. Richard's was slightly longer than Nigel's, but Nigel's seemed fatter, and she knew that whatever happened she was in for a couple of hours of pure pleasure of a sexual nature.

'Undress me,' she said. 'I want to be naked.'

Nigel set the ball rolling by unzipping her dress and she

let the top fall into her lap to expose the camisole beneath. Her breasts felt swollen and sore, and they pushed against the thin silk that covered them. She felt Richard pull the straps off her shoulders and she shrugged the garment down to her waist, exposing the twin orbs of delight to the greedy eyes of her two partners.

Nigel bent down and took one long, hard, red nipple into his mouth and Richard did the same with the other. Danielle was in heaven as they sucked at her teats. She could feel stabs of delight running down to her womb and through the length of her love canal to her clitoris, which felt as if it might burst, so engorged with blood was it.

As the two men fastened themselves to her breasts — like twin babies feasting on their mother's milk — she struggled to push her dress and the camisole over her hips and on to the floor.

As they continued to suck and bite at her tits, their hands moved together under her knickers and pushed the thin strip of the gusset of her G-string aside, until they both had their fingers pushing up inside the wetness of her. She moved on them, until one — she didn't know which — slid his hand up the crack between her buttocks, and wetly pushed one finger into her anus. She cried out as it forced its way into the tiny hole, enlarging it as he went. Danielle was in heaven. Her breasts were being loved, and her cunt, and her arsehole. It was the most intense pleasure she'd ever felt in her life and she wished that it would never end.

She fumbled at their flies, pulling down the zips and reaching inside to find the hot flesh of their manhood. She wanted to be naked with them, and for them to be naked next to her. Piece by piece, they managed to wrestle out of their clothes whilst still playing with her body. Eventually both Nigel and Richard divested themselves of the last stitch that they were wearing, whilst Danielle was still dressed in stockings and suspenders, French knickers, her G-string and high-heeled shoes.

She looked at the two men as they sat next to her with their hands moving all over her body and they both smiled at her reassuringly, and she smiled back.

It was like a dream. A dream of paradise come true. Two men to give her pleasure. Two mouths to lick and kiss her, four hands to play with her body, and best of all, two gigantic, hard pricks, and two pairs of balls filled with sperm, ready to shoot into her defenceless body.

As their hands roamed over her, she took turns in giving them long, deep kisses on their mouths. Sucking out their spit, and tasting the brandy they had all drunk a few minutes before.

As Nigel's and Richard's desire for her grew, the kisses got shorter and Danielle was pulled roughly from one to the other. She loved the way they were treating her. Like a whore. Like a tart brought in for the night, to be discarded in the morning. Like a piece of meat. Merchandise to be used, then thrown away.

As the kisses continued she put both hands down into their laps and played with two cocks at once. Massaging and wanking them and feeling the hard weight of their balls as she gently lifted them and balanced them on the palms of her hands.

She teased at their pubic hair, rubbing her fingers through it just above the skin, knowing the effect that had on men. They both loved it and she could see their cocks jerking up and down as she did it.

Then she went down on them one after the other.

Firstly she bent over Nigel's groin, moving her arse so that Richard could finger her anus under her knickers, and slide his hand down to the tight V of material between her legs that just covered her entrance. She sucked at Nigel's prick with her hot, wet mouth, dribbling her own saliva onto it. Then she sucked it off, pausing only to lick and kiss the length of his knob, and to tease his bollocks with her tongue.

As she serviced his prick, Nigel rubbed her back and neck, and Richard eased her lace pants over her hips, leaving the G-string in place. He went down onto her bottom with his mouth, pulled the thin cord of the tiny garment out of her crack, and ran his tongue along it, drinking down the juice that had dribbled out of her pussy and run down into the gap between her buttocks. Then he forced his tongue into her arsehole. As the hot, wet flesh entered her back passage, she sucked harder at Nigel's dick in her passion.

After a few minutes, like someone faced with a feast after a famine, she tired of that game and pulled away. She turned and stuck her bottom up into her husband's face as she began to devour Richard's prick.

She loved the different tastes of the men, the different shape of their equipment, and the different texture of their skin under her questing tongue.

Whilst she was busy servicing Richard's dong, she felt Nigel's face where Richard's had been not a minute before. He pressed his mouth against her cunt and flicked his tongue against the gusset of her tiny panties. His mouth moved over her pubes in a most delightful way, nibbling at the flesh and hair as he went. Then he tired of seeing anything covering her pussy, and tore the G-string off her body tossing it into the corner of the room. Once Danielle was fully exposed to him, he pushed his tongue right up inside her and explored the inside of her cunt with it.

She loved the freedom of her slit being totally naked, and she opened her legs as wide as she could to allow him easier access. He knew exactly what she wanted and plastered his head hard between her thighs, pushing his tongue so far up her, that she thought it was almost inside her womb. She nearly swooned at the wonderful feeling that his mouth was giving her and slurped even harder on Richard's cock.

Then Nigel pulled his head away, moved around behind her, and she felt his helmet at the entrance to her cunt.

At last, she thought, I'm going to get what I really want.

Nigel's prick slid easily up the soaking length of her and she almost bit a chunk out of Richard's knob as she felt herself being entered from behind by her husband's love machine.

He moved easily on her, taking his time with a slow shag that forced waves of delight through Danielle's belly.

She knew by the way that Nigel was fucking her, that he had no intention of coming quickly and was only interested in giving her pleasure, and she silently thanked him as he slid in and out of her puss with long, slow, deliberate strokes.

She closed her legs on his tool and found his speed with her cunt muscles, trying to squeeze as much satisfaction out of him as she could.

In and out he went, fucking her gently as he watched her suck on another man's prick.

Then he withdrew and pulled her away from Richard's

groin. Reluctantly she allowed her lover's cock to slip out of her mouth and Nigel turned her round so that her arse faced Richard. He accepted the invitation and entered her doggie style from the rear just like Nigel had done.

As his prick entered her, and she put her mouth round Nigel's dick, she was glad they'd decided to get the four seat sofa as it allowed plenty of room for group sex.

Richard's cock moved slowly in and out of her, teasing her pussy, just like Nigel's had done. She wanted the feel of hot sperm bursting inside her but she realised that the two men had made an unspoken pact to tantalise her half to death before giving her the satisfaction she so desperately craved, and – although she wanted relief – the delightful feeling that she was being used simply as a sex object for their carnal desires made her feel weak and feminine, and not in as much control as she had thought she was.

Then Richard also pulled out of her and she felt hollow inside, but not for long.

He lay on his back on the sofa and Danielle climbed on top of him and lowered herself onto his cock. Then Nigel climbed on her too, making her into a sex sandwich, and gently eased his prick into her anus.

She felt as if she might burst with joy. Her whole body was full of cock. She rode Richard as Nigel rode her. Her insides were on fire and she was loving every second.

'Come,' she cried. 'Spunk me, you bastards.' And she ground her hips down on Richard's groin as Nigel rode her back.

Faster and faster they went until, in one huge explosion of sexual energy, her two lovers shot their loads into her and she orgasmed with a wail like a banshee.

30

After their mutual climaxes, the three of them collapsed onto each other in a pile of sweaty, come-spattered limbs. As the two men's penises softened and slid out of Danielle's cunt and arsehole, she felt Richard's and Nigel's jism leaking out of her in a warm, wet stream, dribbling down her legs and dripping off onto whoever was lying beneath her.

She felt totally sated with sex and as pleased as she could remember: proud that she'd managed to satisfy two men, and herself into the bargain.

Nigel was lying on top of her and was the first to move. He dragged himself to his feet, pulled on his trousers and found the brandy bottle and their glasses. He sloshed liquor into them and passed them round like a commanding officer to his exhausted troops after a long and successful battle.

Danielle swigged down a mouthful of the fiery liquid gratefully and then looked at the two men. Richard was sitting naked up against one arm of the sofa. He grinned at her naughtily and raised his glass in a toast. She returned the compliment and then looked up at Nigel. His face was covered with a broad smile too. It had all worked out very well.

'Did you know?' she asked her husband.

'What?'

'About me and Richard.'

He nodded a reply. 'I came home the other afternoon and saw you together.'

'And you weren't angry?'

Nigel reddened then said, 'No. Just the opposite. I rather enjoyed being a Peeping Tom. Has it been going on long?'

'No,' replied Richard. 'That was the first time. I returned the milk I'd borrowed and it just happened. Something clicked.'

Danielle was enjoying the conversation, sitting naked except for her stockings and suspender belt, drinking brandy with the two men who had just serviced her and discussing their sex lives together.

All the men I know seem to like to watch me screwing, she thought, as her mind went back to Laurence looking on as Charles had fucked her. I wonder why?

'I thought as much,' she said, 'from the way you've been acting this last week or so. Why didn't you say anything?'

Nigel shrugged. 'I don't know,' he replied.

'And that was why you wanted Richard to come to dinner tonight. So that we could all do this together?'

Nigel nodded.

'You sly old boots,' said Danielle. She could hardly believe that her strait-laced husband had plotted the whole thing, but the knowledge made her feel extremely sexy. 'Do you want to watch again?' she asked, pushing one nylon-clad foot against Richard's thigh.

Nigel raised his eyebrows. 'I wouldn't mind,' he said.

'Why don't we all go upstairs. I'm sure it can be arranged. What do you think, Richard?' said Danielle.

Richard nodded, his cock already thickening at the thought of another love session with the delectable woman sitting next to him with her legs open, exposing her sex.

'Come on then,' she said, and stood up, feeling even more spunk ooze out of her and slide down to soak her stocking tops as she did so. 'I'm getting horny again thinking about it.'

She reached out her hand to Richard and he took it, rising from where he was sitting to join her. Arm in arm they walked upstairs to the bedroom, with Nigel tagging along behind carrying the brandy bottle in one hand.

When they entered the room, Danielle switched on the bedside lamps and dimmed them to their lowest and most romantic setting, pulled the covers off the bed and lay down. Richard joined her and Nigel sat on the dressing-table stool where he had a perfect view of the bed.

The two lovers kissed, gently at first, and then more passionately as they forgot that they were being watched and began to concentrate on each other.

Danielle could hardly believe she was ready for fucking so soon after a threesome. But she was. Perhaps it was the smell of sex that lingered so strongly on her and Richard's sweaty bodies. Perhaps it was the fact that Nigel knew about one of her affairs. She didn't know and she didn't care. All she did care about was the empty feeling inside her that could only be satisfied one way: to be filled with hot cock and for her to be screwed until she screamed.

And she could tell that Richard was just as eager. His prick stood rampantly away from his body, fully erect again, only twenty minutes after it had come so spectacularly.

She slid her hand down his slick torso, gathered his weapon into her grip and squeezed it tightly as they kissed.

Their mouths seemed to be glued together with desire and they nibbled at each other's lips and tongues in their eagerness to be as close as two people could be. Danielle moved her mouth down to his neck, then slid it further down his chest, through the hair around his nipples and sucked one up into her mouth.

No wonder men like breasts so much, she thought.

Richard moved round her and allowed his face to rove over her shoulders and the top of her back, kissing every inch that he could reach. They were like a pair of romping puppies, writhing over each other, finding new pleasure centres to stroke and lick and caress. From his seat on the stool Nigel looked on entranced as his wife displayed herself in front of him, and a plan began to form somewhere in the back of his mind.

Finally both Richard's and Danielle's mouths found each other's genitals. Richard's cock was musky from being inside her cunt and, as she sucked on the hardness of it, she could smell her own sex on his skin and taste the residue of her own juice that was matted into his pubic hair. She loved luxuriating in her own femininity and breathed in the odour as she worked her lips on his manhood and up into the crack of his arse.

Richard sucked his own jism out of Danielle's cunt and tasted the sharp strangeness of Nigel's sperm that had been deposited in his wife's anus and which was now dribbling down her crack to mix with Richard's and Danielle's own juices to form a thick glue of mutual love.

By now, Richard didn't care whose come he had in his mouth. The woman that he was with made him hornier than any woman he had ever known. The mixture of innocence and carnal knowledge she emanated from every pore just drove him crazy. He didn't care that her husband was watching him roger the wench. There could have been an audience of thousands of strangers present and he would have still done it. His cock was like steel and he felt the sperm bubbling in his balls like boiling water.

'I want to fuck you, my darling,' he cried. 'I want to fill you with spunk.'

Danielle adored it when men spoke like that to her. And the fact of Nigel's presence made it even better.

'Fuck me then,' she said in reply. 'Fill my womb with your love. I need you Richard. I want your come inside me.'

He climbed onto her soft, sweet body and pushed his cock hard against her bush, until she opened like a blossoming flower and accepted his member into the softness of her pussy. Her flesh closed over his and they were as one. He slid easily into her and, as she accepted his prick, it pushed eagerly into her and just as eagerly she pushed her hips back against his loins. He pumped his arse hard down onto her and she opened her legs wide and looped them round his back, crossing her ankles so that she could feel every inch of his thrust as he pounded his muscular body down onto her soft curves.

Danielle looked over at Nigel as she and Richard fucked. Their eyes locked together and she smiled at her husband and blew him a kiss with her lips as Richard beat at her with his cock.

And as she looked, she felt her insides turn to hot liquid, as yet another orgasm swept over her like surf on a beach. As the feeling transported her to heaven, and she faintly heard Richard's own cries of pleasure as he splashed her insides with his semen, she knew that from that day on her life would never be the same again.

31

Danielle and Richard lay closely together, side by side on the bed after their lovemaking, and she watched as Nigel got silently to his feet and left the room.

'You'd better get dressed,' she said to her lover after a few minutes.

'Do you think he's upset?' Richard asked.

'No. But I'd like some time alone with him. I'll get your clothes.'

She got off the bed, slipped into a peach-coloured, silk dressing gown that was hanging on the back of the door and went downstairs. Nigel was in the living room. He had put his shirt back on and was sitting on the sofa drinking from his brandy glass.

Danielle went over and sat next to him, putting her arm round his shoulder. 'Are you all right, darling?' she asked.

'Of course.'

'Not upset?'

'No, not in the least. Just a little surprised at myself.'

'It's been a surprising kind of evening.'

'You can say that again.'

'You're a wonderful man and I *do* love you,' said Danielle, hugging him tightly.

Nigel kissed his wife on the cheek. 'And I love you too,' he said.

'I'll take Richard's clothes upstairs and get rid of him. I think we should talk.'

Nigel nodded and Danielle got up and gathered Richard's stuff together, then went back up to the bedroom closing the living room door behind her as she went.

When she gave them to him, Richard pulled his clothes back on and said, 'Do we meet again?'

'I don't know,' said Danielle. 'We'll have to see.'

'Call me,' he said, and together they went downstairs.

'Make my farewells for me,' said Richard, 'and I hope we can get together soon.'

'Me too,' said Danielle, and kissed him on the cheek before letting him out of the front door.

She went back to the living room where Nigel was still sitting, sipping at his brandy.

Once again she joined him on the sofa. They said nothing for a few minutes before Danielle broke the silence. 'I won't do it again if you don't want me to.'

Nigel turned to her and gathered her up in his arms. 'Just the opposite,' he whispered. 'I loved watching you fucking. It was as if I was watching myself with you.'

She squeezed him tightly. 'I never suspected you'd want to.'

'Nor did I. But I loved it. Have you had many other men since we've been married?'

'No,' she lied. 'Richard was the only one. Why, would you mind?'

'Not if you'd let me watch.'

'Nigel, I'm surprised at you.'

'I'm surprised at myself. If you'd've told me a month

ago that I was a voyeur, I would have denied it emphatically.'

'Is that what you are then? A voyeur?'

'I must be.'

'But you're also a doer, aren't you?'

He nodded and Danielle opened the gown she was wearing. 'Then do me,' she said. 'I want you to wash Richard's seed out of me with yours.'

'Do you? Do you really?'

'Of course,' she said, and opened her legs. 'Come on, darling. Lick him out of me and replace his come with yours.'

Nigel's head went down to her bush and he dipped his tongue into the smelly centre of it where she'd already been fucked three times that night. Her pussy was like a swamp of sex and Nigel lost himself in the delicious tastes and smells of it as he licked round her cunt lips, then drank from the open slit as if it were a goblet of vintage wine. He lapped the liquid that filled it into his mouth and drank it down. Then he followed the silver trails of semen down to where it had dried in her stocking tops and sucked at the white crust on the black nylon.

Danielle lay back and enjoyed being eaten and drunk. She opened herself as widely as possible to his roving tongue and closed her eyes and drifted into a reverie of pure sexual pleasure.

After fifteen minutes of nibbling at her hairy peach, Nigel got up from his knees and removed his shirt and trousers again. Danielle looked at him standing over her and was gratified to see that his manhood was erect once more. She opened her arms in invitation and he joined with her again for another bout of sexual love.

His prick seemed to fill her to bursting point and she lay as far back as she could, so that she was bent almost double and could hook her legs over his shoulders to allow him maximum penetration. Busily, he worked himself off inside her and their mouths met in a the longest, most passionate kiss she could ever remember.

'Was it good?' he breathed into her ear.

'What?'

'Being watched.'

'It was wonderful.'

'What were you thinking about?'

'You my darling,' she replied. 'Only you.'

As she spoke, his movements became faster and more frenzied. 'Is his cock like mine?' he asked breathlessly.

'Not as good,' said Danielle. 'Not as loving.'

'Mine's the best, then?'

'The best in the world. Now flush him out of me with your come. Wash him away. Make me forget all about him.'

'Will you?'

'If you fuck me better than he did.'

Nigel beat at her with his body to make her wish come true and she beat back at him with her own, until the only sound in the room was the harshness of their breathing and the slapping sound as their bellies met and parted.

'Shoot me darling,' she cried. 'Shoot me hard, I'm going to come.'

And she was. She could feel the heat in her cunt moving up through her womb, towards her breasts. She couldn't believe she could come again so quickly, but miraculously she was. And she was loving every second of it. Nigel's sweat-soaked body was pulling another orgasm from her and she rode it like a roller coaster. Up and down, until finally she knew she was on the edge of ecstasy. She stayed suspended there for as long as she could, before the wave broke and she pulled her husband so close to her that she could feel his heart beating on hers, and, as he shot his load up her, she felt the vortex of the sexual spasm fling her to heaven.

32

Danielle and Nigel spent the following day in bed together, on the dirty sheets where Danielle had been fucked the night before and that Nigel had refused to let her change. He'd told her that making love on them made him horny. And if the truth be known, it made her horny too.

That day they couldn't seem to get enough of each other. Danielle had never realised that her husband was capable of such passion, and hers matched his completely. Finally, on Sunday evening, they lay exhausted together in each other's arms, kissing and caressing.

'You haven't forgotten about Wednesday?' he asked between kisses.

'Wednesday . . .?'

'The firm's dance.'

'God, I had. Where is it again?'

'At that new hotel near Gatwick. It's supposed to be very grand.'

'I'll need a new dress.'

'Then buy one. Nothing but the best for the sales manager's wife. And new underwear to go with it, if you like.'

'Can I? How lovely. I haven't had a new dress for . . .'

'Weeks, at least,' Nigel said.

'Oh Nigel, don't tease me.'

He kissed her again and she felt his hardness against her once more.

'Who's going to be there?' she asked.

'Everyone. From the top to the bottom. From the great and the good to the tea boy.'

'Sounds like fun. Is that dirty old man Guggenheim going to make an appearance?'

'The big boss? Of course.'

'I hope he doesn't try and touch me up again.'

'Danielle,' said Nigel sternly. 'You *have* to be nice to him. He's very important to my career.'

'How nice?'

'As nice as possible.'

'Nigel, you don't want me to . . .?'

He silenced her with a kiss, then said, 'Just be nice to him. For my sake. For *our* sakes.'

And with those words Danielle knew that she'd been right in what she'd thought when Nigel had been watching her fuck Richard: her life would never be the same again.

She couldn't stand Guggenheim. He was old and fat and greasy, and she was sure he didn't wash very often. And on every previous occasion that they'd met, he'd made it patently obvious that he'd love to get inside Danielle's knickers and ransack the delicate and precious contents that he'd find there.

So that's what it's all about Nigel, she thought. A straight swap. Your wife's favours for a cushy job at HQ. Oh dear, what is the world coming to?

'And don't forget I'm away all next weekend,' Nigel went on. 'But I'm sure you won't be lonely,' and there was an unpleasant leer in his voice as he said it.

You can count on it, thought Danielle. Lately I've found that I need never be lonely at all.

33

On Monday morning, bright and early, Danielle went up to the West End and spent a fortune on a new party frock. It was made of navy blue, shot silk, was cut daringly low at the back, seemed to defy gravity as it hung off her braless breasts at the front, and the skirt was very short and tight.

I look like a right little tart, she thought, as she surveyed herself in the full-length mirror of the Bond Street shop where she purchased the outfit. But then, that's exactly what Nigel wants me to look like, and I'd hate to disappoint him.

To complete the ensemble, she purchased a tiny, pale blue, silk G-string, a pair of dark blue, seamed, hold-up stockings, and some very high-heeled shoes that perfectly matched the colour of the dress. Very pleased with her shopping trip, and with her bank account in tatters, she returned home and hung the dress in her wardrobe.

When Nigel asked if her shopping spree had been a success she answered in the affirmative, but when he asked to see the outfit she told him it was a secret and he must wait until Wednesday evening.

On Tuesday afternoon Laurence called her on the phone.

'Long time no see,' he said, when she answered.

'I told you I didn't like you calling me at home,' she said.

'How else could I get in touch? Don't be cross. I called at this time because I thought your husband would be at work. But if a man had answered I'd've pretended it was a wrong number.'

'So what do you want?' asked Danielle.

'I don't suppose you're free on Saturday evening.'

'I don't suppose I am. Why?'

'I thought we might get together.'

'What, just you, me and Charlie?'

Laurence laughed down the line. 'No. Just you and me. I've been invited to a party. I need a partner.'

'And you thought of me? I'm flattered. But I don't think so.'

'That's a shame,' replied Laurence. 'It would be the ideal opportunity for us to meet again.'

'I'm sure it would. But I'm equally sure you'll find someone to go with. I expect there are dozens of women queuing up to be with you for an evening.'

'Sarcasm doesn't suit you my dear Danielle. I don't care who's queuing up. It's you I want to take, and you alone. Are you sure you can't come?'

Danielle hesitated. She knew that Nigel was away all weekend and she had no plans of her own.

'Where is the party?'

'Mayfair. It's going to be a very swish affair. Everyone will be there. Do come.'

'Let me think about it. I'll call you on Thursday. Is that all right?'

'It'll have to be. Do try to get away. I would like to see you again.'

I just bet you would, thought Danielle as she replaced the receiver on the cradle after they had said their farewells.

Nigel took his evening clothes to work with him on Wednesday. The plan was that he'd get ready there – then because the company didn't want any of their top executives pulled up on the way home and breathalysed – a chauffeur driven car would pick up Danielle at home, collect Nigel at his office, and then they'd both be driven down to Gatwick where the car would wait until they were ready to leave.

That suited Danielle perfectly, as it would give her the run of the bathroom all afternoon and Nigel wouldn't see her new outfit until she could make a grand entrance.

At about three, she ran a deep, hot, foamy bath and luxuriated in it for more than an hour. She'd been to the hairdressers in the morning for a trim and after her bath she simply washed and dried her hair, leaving it to fall to her shoulders in a most natural and attractive way. She spent another hour on her make-up and doused herself in her favourite perfume, Joy, before getting her new dress out of the wardrobe.

She held it up in front of her and look in the bedroom mirror. Perfect, she thought. This little number will cause a sensation tonight.

She laid it on the bed and undid the bag that contained her new underwear.

First of all she pulled the skimpy G-string over her hips. The tiny V of smooth silk at the front fitted snugly over her hairy mound and the string at the back ran up the crack between her buttocks.

Then she sat down and carefully pulled on her new

stockings. She stood up and checked that the seams were straight before climbing into the dress. It was a miracle of the dressmaker's art. It clung to her perfect figure as if it had been made for her. She smoothed it down and admired herself once more in the mirror. The dress was like a second skin and her underwear was so brief that she might not have been wearing any at all. In fact it looked as if she wasn't.

No VPL there, she thought, as she did a twirl and checked her reflection.

Finally, she stepped into her new shoes, put a light coat over her outfit, picked up her handbag and, as she was walking downstairs the doorbell rang; the chauffeur had arrived.

They collected Nigel from his office in Croydon. When he came out through the glass doors at the front of the building, Danielle thought how handsome he looked in his dinner suit, starched white shirt and black bow tie. And when he got in the car, she pulled him close, kissed him, and told him so.

'Thank you,' he said. 'You smell beautiful. Let's have a look at this dress then.'

But Danielle pulled her coat closely around her and told him that he'd have to wait a little longer before he was allowed to get a peek.

'Well, I hope it's worth the wait,' said Nigel.

'I hope so too, darling,' replied his wife. 'It certainly cost enough.'

Nigel smiled, tapped on the partition, and the driver pulled away. They were soon speeding down the motorway towards Gatwick.

When they arrived at the hotel where the dinner was

being held, Danielle vanished into the ladies cloakroom to leave her coat and check her make-up. While she was gone, Nigel waited in the reception area.

She stood just inside the doorway of the ladies, smoothed down the tight material of her skirt once more, checked herself for the umpteenth time in the mirror, and finally made her grand entrance.

Nigel's reaction was *indeed* worth the wait, as was the effort that Danielle had made with her appearance. When he saw his wife for the first time in her new outfit, his eyes almost popped out of his head.

'That's a sensational dress,' he said, when she had made her way across to where he was standing, gathering admiring glances from every side as she went. 'My God, darling, you look like a film star.'

'I'm glad you like it,' replied Danielle, 'and I wonder if old Guggenheim, your esteemed chairman and managing director will like it too. After all, I'm only dolled up like this for his benefit, just as you wanted me to be. I hope you won't change your mind when you see the bill.'

'Whatever it cost, it was worth it,' Nigel said. 'Every penny.'

When they went into the bar for pre-dinner drinks, all heads turned – both male and female – at their entrance to look at Danielle. She was far and away the best looking, and most glamorous woman in the room. She and Nigel took a table in one corner and three waiters were immediately buzzing round them to take their order.

Danielle chose a white wine spritzer and Nigel asked for a bottle of imported lager.

As soon as the waiters had gone, other male members of the firm gravitated towards the table as if it were a magnet. Some of them Danielle knew, and others were strangers that Nigel introduced to her. They all complimented Danielle on how she looked and she thought that she had never previously been the object of so much naked lust from so many men. Amongst them was Roger Clinton, one of Danielle's conquests from the memorable weekend in Southampton. He shook Nigel's hand warmly and took Danielle's in his own for rather too long.

'It so good to see you again,' he said to both of them, but she knew that the words were really for her alone. 'Mrs Morgan, may I say you look absolutely delightful tonight?'

'Of course you may,' said Danielle, lowering her eyelashes demurely as she remembered his cock thrusting inside her on the back seat of his BMW. 'And it's still Danielle. I thought we'd gone past those formalities when you and your wife had dinner with us in Southampton. Where is she, by the way?'

'At the bar,' replied Roger. 'Will you come and join us for a drink?'

'Bring her over here,' said Nigel. 'Let's make up a foursome. I'd be delighted to see her again.'

Roger left to fetch his wife and Nigel said to Danielle, 'You're certainly causing a stir here. I don't think they've ever seen anyone as beautiful as you.'

Danielle smiled. 'Why thank you, darling,' she said. 'I'm simply trying to please my lord and master.'

'You're succeeding,' said Nigel.

A moment later, Roger Clinton returned with this wife. She was wearing a little black dress and pearls and, although it was obvious she had taken a great deal of care with her appearance, next to Danielle she looked rather ordinary.

'You remember Anne, don't you,' said Roger.

Nigel stood up, took her right hand in both of his and kissed her lightly on the cheek. 'Of course I do. I hope we'll get a chance of another dance later. And you remember my wife Danielle, don't you Anne?'

'How could I forget?' said Anne Clinton, shooting Danielle a dirty look. She still wasn't sure what had gone on between her husband and Danielle on the Saturday evening when they'd last met, even though Roger had sworn that nothing untoward had occurred, and the scarlet silk panties that she'd found under the back seat of his car must have been left there as a practical joke by his colleagues at work. But whatever *had* happened, she was still aware that Danielle Morgan *was* her husband's boss's wife, and thus a very important person that she had to be pleasant to, so she shook Danielle's hand politely and said, 'I love your dress Mrs Morgan. You make the rest of us look dowdy by comparison.'

'Nonsense,' said Danielle, catching the drift of what was going on in an instant, and putting on one of her best insincere smiles. 'You look lovely. And please do call me Danielle, Anne.'

Anne Clinton smiled in return, but her smile was just as false as Danielle's.

Totally unaware of what was going on, Nigel seated Anne and Roger Clinton, and called for more drinks.

As the next half hour passed, their table was the most popular in the room and, until the announcement was made that dinner was served, no end of people stopped by to say hello.

Finally, at about seven thirty, the maitre d' opened the doors to the restaurant and the people in the crowded bar made their way in to dinner.

Sir George Guggenheim and his wife Melissa were waiting inside the door to greet them.

It was a custom that the chairman left his employees to enjoy their pre-dinner drinks without his formidable presence, so that they could relax and chat together before he welcomed them into the dining room.

Sir George was a mountain of a man in every way. At sixty-six years old, he stood easily six foot four inches tall, and was every ounce of twenty stone in weight. Although it was known that he was as rich as Croesus, he still worked a fifteen hour day, seven days a week. And he ran the company that he had built up from a wireless repair shop in the back room of his parent's house in Dalston to the massive multinational electronics conglomerate that it was now, with a rod of iron. He was famous for his bad moods, meanness, prodigious appetites in all things – especially food, drink and young blonde women – but his charisma was such that his staff were totally loyal.

As that very same staff and their partners began to filter through from the bar, he took the arm of his wife – ten years his junior and a quarter of his size, who looked like a wizened stick insect next to him – and moved forward to greet them one by one.

He noticed Danielle straight away as she waited her turn to shake his hand, and he felt his libido come to the fore at the sight of her. He'd always had a fancy for Nigel Morgan's wife and the way she looked that particular night almost took his breath away. Previously she'd always politely rebuffed his advances, but Sir George hadn't got where he was by accepting rejection and he wondered if tonight might be a different story.

Although there were several hundred people in the bar,

Sir George seemed to know them all by name and had a word for each of them. But it was Nigel and Danielle that he spoke to longest, holding her hand in his for almost a minute as he greeted them.

His boss's interest in his wife was not lost on Nigel. It was exactly what he wanted. The plan that had occurred to him as he watched her fuck Richard in their bed four days earlier, was finally coming to fruition. He wanted the chairman in his pocket, and one way that he might attain his goal was for the old goat to get inside Danielle's panties. Nigel knew that once Sir George had her, he'd want her again and again, and if there was a slight price to be paid, Nigel was sure that Sir George would be glad to pay it.

The attention that Nigel's boss was paying to her wasn't lost on Danielle either. She'd had a pretty good idea what was in Nigel's mind and when she saw the look on his face as the older man grasped her hand in his sweaty paw, she knew she'd been right.

Not that she cared. Lately she didn't seem to care about very much. Except fucking. And if Nigel wanted her to open her legs for the old scoundrel in front of her, well, so be it. But she had to confess that deep in her heart of hearts she was disappointed in her husband.

She smiled up at Sir George as he spoke to her. 'Mrs Morgan,' he said. 'I'd be the envy of every man present, if you would do me the honour of saving the first dance for me after dinner. I beg of you to say you will.'

'Do call me Danielle, Sir George,' she said, then looked at Lady Melissa Guggenheim standing in her husband's shadow. She was wearing a Versace dress that must have cost four times as much as Danielle's, but looked like a limp rag next to it. 'And of course I'd be delighted. That is, if your wife doesn't mind.'

Lady Guggenheim gritted her teeth and smiled at the younger woman. She refused to allow one iota of the jealousy she felt for Danielle to show on her face – a face that had been lifted so often it was surprising that her nostrils weren't in the middle of her forehead.

'Of course not my dear,' she said with a warmth she didn't feel. 'It's only correct that the most handsome man in the room should have the first dance with the most beautiful woman here.'

'If that were true then Sir George would be dancing with you, Lady Guggenheim,' said Nigel with a smarmy smile. 'But in his absence may I offer myself as a most unworthy partner to *you* for the first dance, as my wife will be otherwise engaged.'

Lady Guggenheim inclined her head in his direction. 'You flatter me, Mr Morgan. But I'd be delighted to accept your *gallant* invitation. You may collect me when the music begins.'

'It will be a pleasure,' said Nigel, and he and Danielle moved on to find their places at their table.

'Dirty old man,' said Danielle when they were seated.

'He likes you.'

'I know he does.'

'Well, keep him happy and I'll take care of *her*.'

'If you say so darling,' she replied, but deep down inside she felt terribly sad that this was what her marriage had come to.

34

The dinner came and went in a blur of rich food, wine, coffee and liqueurs, followed by too many long speeches. But eventually, by nine-thirty, the meal was over and the doors to the main ballroom of the hotel were flung open so that the real business of the evening could begin: dancing, drinking, and flirting, as the employees of Guggenheim International Electronics Inc, began to let their back hair down.

Sir George went to the bandstand and appropriated the microphone.

'Ladies and gentlemen,' he said, 'I'll keep this very short as I'm sure you've all had quite enough of speeches for one evening. All I will say is the bar is open and the drinks are free. The band will play until the last guest leaves, but tomorrow is a working day and I'll expect a doctor's note at the very least in case of any absenteeism.'

The announcement was met by jeers, whistles and catcalls. It was another custom that the day after the firm's dance was the only day of the year, except for bank holidays and Christmas day, when the offices of Guggenheim Inc were almost deserted.

'So enjoy yourself, my loyal friends,' he went on. 'This has been another record year for us and you deserve my thanks once again. So let the fun begin and let's hope that the year that starts the day after tomorrow is another record breaker.'

With that, he tossed the mike to the band leader and hopped off the stage with an agility that was surprising in a man of his bulk. As the band began to play, he made for Danielle who was standing next to Nigel and Lady Melissa.

'The first dance, as promised,' Sir George said, as he took Danielle's hand.

'Of course, Sir George,' she replied, as she went into his arms.

'And my wife with your husband. How appropriate.' he continued, as Lady Melissa and Nigel followed suit. The four of them moved towards the centre of the floor and only then did the other employees, and their husbands and wives, girlfriends and boyfriends, fiancées and lovers, pair up and join them.

Sir George pulled Danielle close as the music took them and she could smell the sharpness of his body odour in her nostrils. But where once it had repelled her, now it was oddly attractive.

As they moved together to the rhythm. Danielle was surprised how good he was and she lost herself in the music as he led her around the floor.

'You're a very good dancer,' he said. 'And it's rare that I get such a tall partner.'

'Thank you,' said Danielle demurely. She felt Sir George Guggenheim pull her closer and she relaxed even more in his embrace.

When the first tune ended, they stood and applauded the band before they struck up the second number.

'Another?' said Sir George.

'I'd love to,' said Danielle, and they waited for the music to start again.

The second song was slower and when Sir George took Danielle in his arms once more and pulled her closer, she was suddenly aware that his member was erect against her belly. He appeared to be not in the least embarrassed as they moved together, as if it was perfectly natural for a man to show his appreciation of a beautiful woman dancing close to him.

His prick felt enormous to Danielle. She enjoyed the feeling as it pressed against her and after a moment she pressed herself back against it. Sir George smiled down at her. 'We should get to know each other better, my dear,' he said. 'I know that young Nigel is going to go far with the company. In fact he's up for a promotion, even as we speak.'

'He's said nothing to me about it,' said Danielle.

The sneak, she thought. So that's what all this is about. I'm to be the sacrificial lamb to this old sod's advances so that my loving husband can *advance* himself. Too bad I'm quite enjoying being the sacrifice. Especially as it's putting so many other people's noses out of joint: because as she and Sir George were dancing, Danielle couldn't avoid noticing the envious glances from some of the other people present who obviously thought it should be their wives dancing with the guv'nor, or in the case of the females, themselves.

'He's far too clever to count his chickens,' replied the older man, 'until I've decided how many will be hatched. I think you I should talk about it. Maybe we could have a drink later.'

'If you like.'

'I do. How about at eleven on the balcony outside. We'll get some air and relax.'

'That sounds perfect,' said Danielle.

35

With that, Sir George led Danielle back to where Nigel and Lady Melissa were waiting. 'Your wife's an excellent dancer, my boy,' boomed the older man. 'Gold medal standard if I'm not far wrong.'

'Thank you, Sir George,' said Nigel. 'And Lady Melissa tells me that you two have won some medals of your own.'

'In the past,' said Sir George. 'We're a little out of practice these days. But I intend to rectify that by having the next dance with her and leaving you two young things alone. Come my dear,' and he took Lady Melissa's hand, leading her back onto the crowded dance floor.

'How did it go?' asked Nigel.

'Very well. You didn't tell me you were going for a promotion.'

'Did he mention it? Excellent. What did he say?'

'He said you were "in line" for it. And he wants to chat to me about it later.'

'Wonderful,' said Nigel. 'When.'

'At eleven on the balcony outside.'

'You must go. Make up to the old boy. I could use a friend like him right now.'

Is that all you care about? thought Danielle sadly. But she smiled and said. 'Don't worry. I'm sure I can twist him round my little finger if needs be.'

The dancing and drinking continued, and by five to eleven the ballroom was hot and noisy. With a wink at Nigel, Danielle slipped away in the direction of the exit that led to where she'd arranged to meet Sir George. Outside it was cool and quiet and the balcony itself was only dimly lit, but the moon was full and bright and Danielle could see her way clearly. She walked around the side of the building and in one corner she saw the silhouette of the unmistakable bulk of her husband's boss leaning against a stone balustrade. She walked over and said quietly, 'Hello again.'

Sir George turned to greet her. 'Danielle,' he said. 'I wondered if you'd be able to get away.'

'Of course. Your wish is my command, Sir George.'

The older man chuckled. 'That's exactly the way the wife of a loyal employee should speak. Would you care for a drink?' And from behind his back he produced a bottle of champagne and two glasses.

'I'd love one,' said Danielle, and expertly he opened the bottle and filled the glasses to the brim. He passed one to Danielle and they clinked the rims together.

'To the future,' said Sir George as they did so.

'Whatever it may bring,' echoed Danielle, and she saw him smile wolfishly in the dim light as he sipped at the wine.

He refilled their glasses and suggested that they take a stroll.

'If my shoes will stand it,' replied Danielle.

'I'm sure they will,' said Sir George, and offered her his arm which she took.

They walked together down the few steps that led into the grounds of the hotel and Sir George led her along a path away from the building. The path was uneven and Danielle was forced to hold on to his arm tightly to keep her balance.

After a few minutes they came to a summer house in the centre of a clearing. On the verandah outside was a padded swing.

'Shall we?' said Sir George.

Danielle nodded in the moonlight, and they went up the wooden stairs to the verandah and sat together on the swing. Then for the third time, Sir George filled their glasses.

By now Danielle was feeling very light headed from all the drinks she'd had at the party and when Sir George put down the bottle, turned and took her in his arms she didn't protest. His lips met hers, and he pushed his fat tongue into her mouth, which she opened to receive it gratefully.

His hands roamed across her body as they kissed. She felt no shame as he pushed up her short skirt and found naked flesh between her stockings and the tiny G-string she was wearing. Just the opposite. The alcohol had inflamed her passion. She was feeling empty inside and wanted to be made complete by a man.

The kiss seemed to last forever; their lips moving on each other's with lust and their tongues shooting in and out of each other's mouths.

Daringly, Danielle put her hand into Sir George's lap. She wanted to know if his cock was really as big as it had felt when he pushed it against her whilst they were dancing. It was. It reared against the material of his trousers like a caged animal and she unzipped his fly to allow it the freedom it needed. It rose through the gap like a colossus of flesh. Danielle had never dreamed that any man could be that big. It stood up from Sir George's body like a flagpole made of hot flesh and Danielle pulled away from the kiss to look at it.

'It's so big,' she said in wonder.

'Do you like it?' asked Sir George.

'It's beautiful.'

'Do you want it?'

'Will it fit?'

'Of course.'

'Will it hurt me?'

'There's only one way to find out.'

Danielle stood up and pulled her skirt up round her waist. Then she pushed the tiny gusset of her G-string to one side and mounted Sir George as he lay back on the seat of the swing. The helmet of his knob was huge, but the lips of her vagina were soaking after the kisses they had shared and as they slid over his cock they opened wide and allowed it access. Danielle felt herself slide down it as if it were greased. At first she thought she was going to burst and pain shot up through her body. But then her love tunnel stretched like elastic, and in a moment the pain was gone and only pleasure remained. After a breathless second she began to ride Sir George's monster prick. As she moved, the swing gently swung beneath them and the rocking movement made the sex even more pleasurable.

As she moved faster, so the swing swung harder, and her faint cries of pleasure were echoed by the squeaking of the chains that attached the seat to the frame. She bounced on Sir George's groin and closed her eyes in concentration as her cunt muscles relaxed and tightened around his vast member. Harder she went, and harder still, until with a guttural cry he released his sperm into her pussy and the hot, thick spunk burst up into her womb and coated the insides of it like paint. She felt herself teeter on the edge of the pit of an orgasm, and milked the last drops of jism out of him until, with the final ejaculation, the tickle she was feeling in her belly became a spasm, and then a flood, and she came too, falling on to his chest, calling out his name in passion as she did.

36

Danielle and Sir George Guggenheim stayed joined at the groin for several minutes, until he lifted her off his prick and laid her next to him on the swing. He was incredibly strong and she felt like a doll in his arms. Sir George got to his feet, put his monster weapon back into his trousers and buttoned himself up. 'We'd better be getting back,' he said.

Danielle roused herself and pulled her skirt down over her knickers which were saturated with his spunk. She stood up and felt the juice gush out of her crack and run down her legs. She rubbed her thighs together, smoothed the material of her dress and took Sir George's arm again for the walk back to the hotel.

'That was wonderful,' she said, as she squeezed his biceps.

'And for me. I hope your husband appreciates the kind of woman he's married to.'

'I'm sure he does,' said Danielle.

'Perhaps we can meet again soon. But in more comfortable surroundings, where I can explore your talents to their full.'

'I hope so too, Sir George.' said Danielle.

When they got back to the balcony Danielle said, 'I'd

better run to the ladies, I must look a mess.'

Sir George looked down at her from his great height and replied, 'Not at all, my dear. You look ravishing. But that's not a bad idea. Maybe it will be better for all concerned if we don't go inside together.'

With a brief kiss on the cheek from Danielle they parted and she went straight to the rest room. In fact she didn't look too bad at all, she thought, and a few seconds with her cosmetic bag got her looking as if nothing untoward had happened.

Randy old bastard, she thought as she looked at herself in the mirror. But that cock. What a beauty. I must have it again.

When she was presentable once more, she went off to find Nigel. He was in the bar with some of his salesmen, but as soon as he saw Danielle enter he broke away, intercepted her and steered her towards a vacant table.

'How did it go?' he asked.

Sitting there next to him with Sir George's jism gluing her thighs together as it dried, Danielle smiled and said. 'Fine.'

'Good. I won't ask you what went on.'

'Nothing much. We just talked.'

Nigel smiled wolfishly again. 'I just bet you did,' he said.

Danielle shrugged. 'But I think you've probably got your promotion,' she said.

'Good,' said Nigel.

Meanwhile, Sir George was getting ready to leave the party. His cock felt satisfied after his brief liaison with Danielle and he was growing tired of the heat and noise.

'What a nice boy that Nigel Morgan is,' said Lady Melissa to her husband. 'A real credit to the company.'

'Yes,' agreed Sir George. 'But that wife of his seems to have turned into a bit of a tart. I had plans to give him a promotion until I talked to her.'

'I shouldn't worry about her,' said Lady Melissa, thinking about how it had felt when Nigel held her in his arms as they danced and the thrill she'd felt in her belly as he'd had led her round the floor. She liked young men around her to pander to her own sexual predilections. Especially young men who worked for Guggenheim Electronics and who she could offer certain favours in exchange for the favours she desired from them. She smiled as she thought of the plans that *she* had for Nigel. 'I think a promotion would be the making of both of them,' she said.

'Hmm,' said Sir George. 'If you think so dear.'

'I do George,' she replied. 'I certainly do.'

After the Guggenheims left, the party continued until the small hours of the morning. Finally Danielle and Nigel climbed into their chauffeur driven car and were sped back to London, where they collapsed into bed and slept the sleep of the very drunk.

The next day, Nigel didn't go into work until after lunch, and when he came home, he was ecstatic.

'We've been invited to Sir George's place in the country, the weekend after next,' he said when he got in.

'Really,' said Danielle. 'What brought that on?'

'I don't know,' he replied. 'But there was a message waiting with my secretary when I got in. It looks like you were right. I am going to get that promotion. Sir George always asks people over to stay the weekend when he's about to bump them up the pecking order.'

'I told you so,' said Danielle.

'I don't know what you did to the old boy,' said Nigel, 'but keep on doing it when we get down there.'

'You want me to fuck him, you mean?'

'Whatever it takes. I don't care.'

And suddenly Danielle realised that he didn't. All he did care about was himself and his career, and the thought saddened her.

'Is my bag packed for the weekend?' asked Nigel, not realising how much he'd hurt his wife.

'Yes,' said Danielle.

'I'll be back on Sunday night. Don't do anything I wouldn't when I'm away.'

Danielle remembered Laurence's invitation to a party on Saturday night and smiled back at her husband. 'I won't,' she said. 'Don't worry.'

After Nigel had left for his business weekend on Friday morning, Danielle cleaned up the house and went shopping. After lunch she telephoned Laurence who answered on the second ring. 'I thought you weren't going to call me yesterday,' he said.

'Sorry. I hope I haven't left it too late to accept your invitation for tomorrow evening.'

'No. I'm glad you can make it. It should be interesting. It always is when I see you.'

'I aim to please,' said Danielle.

'You do. The party starts at nine. Shall I collect you?'

'No,' said Danielle. 'I'll drive up to your place.'

'Please yourself,' said Laurence. 'Put on your best frock

and call for me any time after eight.'

'I'll see you at eight then,' said Danielle, and put down the phone with a satisfied look on her face.

37

On Saturday, Danielle took all afternoon to get ready for the party. She knew that she was going to be fucked before the night was out and dressed accordingly. She put on a tight black dress – fastened at the back with hooks and eyes – over a black, strapless, push-up bra, black knickers that were no more than two triangles of silk connected with elastic, a black suspender belt that held up sheer, seamed black stockings and a pair of wickedly high-heeled, black patent leather shoes. She spent an inordinately long time on her make-up, especially around her eyes, which she coated heavily with mascara. When she was ready, she looked in the mirror in her bedroom and was well pleased with the result.

She put a dark coat over the outfit and left the house.

She drove to Laurence's house in Clapham, where she left her car, before being driven in his Jaguar to Mayfair.

The penthouse where the party was being held was in a purpose-built block overlooking Hyde Park.

In the lift that swept them to the top floor, Laurence explained that the party was being given by a fabulously rich American film producer, who was in London to make a big budget porno movie for an independent Hollywood studio.

'I hope I'm not expected to perform,' said Danielle.

'Don't worry, love,' replied Laurence. 'The thing has already been cast. But there's someone I want you to meet. Lilith O'Hara. She runs a model agency and she's always looking for new talent.'

'I think I'm a bit old for that,' replied Danielle. 'The models I see these days seem to be hardly into their teens.'

'Whatever,' said Laurence. 'Anyway, she's quite a woman. I think you'll like her.'

The penthouse was a designer's dream. The furniture was upholstered in real Zebra skin, the drapes were pure silk and the off-white carpets had such deep pile that, high heels or not, it almost came up to Danielle's ankles.

The Beatles White album was oozing gently from an invisible sound system when they exited the lift and a uniformed maid took Danielle's coat.

'You look beautiful in that dress,' said Laurence. 'On second thoughts maybe you could get a part in the film.'

Danielle shook her head, but secretly she was flattered by Laurence's remark.

The film producer was fat and forty, dressed in a leather jacket, jeans, basketball boots and a baseball cap, and he had a long unlit cigar in his mouth at an aggressive angle.

'Hi Laurie,' he said, when he spotted Laurence. 'How they hangin'?'

'Can't complain Josh,' replied Laurence. 'I'd like you to meet a friend of mine. A very good friend. Danielle Morgan. Danielle, this is Josh Steinbeck. Josh – Danielle.'

Josh enveloped Danielle's right hand in both of his. 'Nice to meetcha,' he said. 'Any friend of Laurie's . . . Welcome to the party. Enjoy. *Mi casa, su casa*, as the hispanics say. There's a bar through there.' He indicated an open door with his thumb. 'And food in the dining room. And Laurie, I'd like to see you pronto, OK?'

'Sure Josh,' replied Laurence. 'Just let us get a drink and I'll be right with you.'

Laurence and Danielle moved through to the next room where a bar had been set up under the control of two professional barmen. Laurence ordered a scotch on the rocks and Danielle asked for a white wine spritzer.

'Some place,' said Danielle as they waited for their drinks to be served.

'A little *louche* for me,' said Laurence. 'But the yanks expect it.'

They collected their glasses and stood for a moment, before Laurence said, 'There's Lilith now.'

Danielle turned and saw a tall woman of about forty with long dark hair enter the room, followed by a young man of no more than Danielle's age. The woman was big breasted, with wide hips, and her hour-glass figure had been shoehorned into a low cut, dark green silk dress, which she wore with black nylons and dark green shoes with heels as high as Danielle's own. On the ring finger of her right hand was a diamond as big as a light bulb, and about as bright, set in a gold mounting.

'She looks expensive,' said Danielle, 'if that rock she's wearing is real.'

'It is,' replied Laurence. 'And you're right, she is.'

He caught the woman's eye and she came over with the young man in tow.

'Laurence,' she cried, when she arrived. 'How are you? It's been far too long,' and she swooped upon him, kissing the air an inch away from both his cheeks.

'Lilith, my dear,' said Laurence. 'You're looking as

wonderful as ever. Allow me to introduce you to Danielle Morgan. Remember I talked about her on the telephone?'

'Of course,' said Lilith, and turned to Danielle with a big-toothed smile. 'She's delightful. Just as you described her.' And she embraced Danielle, kissing her on the cheek. As she did so Danielle was enveloped in a cloud of expensive perfume.

Surprised by the effusiveness of the greeting, Danielle said, 'A pleasure.'

'And this is Dominic,' Lilith said, introducing her companion, rather as an afterthought.

He was a dissolute-looking individual with a fringe of dark hair that he kept flicking out of his eyes. He looked at Danielle admiringly and said with a cut-glass accent, ''Delighted, I'm sure.' Then he shook Laurence's hand and said, 'Lilith, a drink?'

'The usual,' replied Lilith. 'Large.'

Dominic went to the bar and Laurence said, 'Lilith. May I leave Danielle with you for a few minutes. I have to speak to Josh right away. Protect the old investment, you know?'

'Of course,' replied Lilith, and Laurence took his drink and made for the door.

When he was gone Lilith said, 'Why don't I get rid of Dom and we can have a long chat Danielle. I'm sure we can find lots to talk about.'

Danielle smiled in assent and when Dominic returned carrying two glasses, giving one to Lilith, she said, 'Dominic darling. Danielle and I want to have girls' talk. Why don't you disappear and find a playmate? I'm sure there's got to be some coke around here that's got your name on it.'

'Of course,' said Dominic, and he excused himself and left the two women alone.

'You've got him very well trained, I must say,' said Danielle.

'It's my only rule with men,' replied Lilith. 'I'm the boss. Now Danielle. Down to business. As Laurence may have told you, I run a very high-class model agency. I supply companions and escorts for gentlemen of quality. And when I spoke to him on the telephone the other day, he mentioned that you were just the kind of girl I could use. And now that I've met you I have to say that everything he said was true.'

So that was it, thought Danielle. Bloody cheek.

'What exactly *did* he say?' she asked.

'That you were beautiful and sexy, but with that something extra that sets you apart from all the other beautiful, sexy girls I see.'

'What kind of something extra?'

'If I knew that, I'd've bottled it and could have retired years ago. So what do you say? My gentlemen come with the finest references and I guarantee full security for my girls. And believe me with looks and style like yours, you could make a great deal of money in a very short time.'

A few weeks earlier, such a suggestion would have horrified Danielle. But since she'd discovered her sexuality, and realised what an effect it had on other people, she could take the offer without turning a single hair on her beautiful head. Nevertheless she said, 'I don't think so Lilith. Thank you for the offer. But I'm a married woman, and besides I don't need the money.'

Lilith smiled in return. 'I'm sorry to hear you say that, and I hope you didn't mind me being so blunt. But I've discovered one thing in my life: that if you don't ask you don't get.'

'Not at all,' said Danielle in reply. 'I admire your honesty and, like I say, I'm flattered.'

'Good,' said Lilith. 'But I warn you, I don't take no for an answer easily. If you change your mind, please give me a call.' She opened her handbag and reached in and took out a card. 'Here's my number in case you do. And even if you don't, please call me anyway. We could have lunch.'

Danielle took the card, opened her own bag and dropped it inside. 'I'd like that.'

'Well, so much for business,' said Lilith, and raised her glass. 'I think we should have a few more drinks and enjoy the party.'

Danielle returned the salute. 'I think you're right,' she agreed.

Over the next half an hour or so, the party began to liven up and the noise level of the music and conversation increased. Eventually Laurence came back into the bar and joined Danielle and Lilith. Then Dominic reappeared and took Lilith off to meet some friends he'd found.

'Did you and Lilith have a nice chat?' asked Laurence when he and Danielle were alone.

'Yes,' replied Danielle. 'But I don't know if I liked you trying to sell me as a high-class whore.'

'You have all the qualifications,' replied Laurence unashamedly. 'And I thought you'd enjoy the work.'

Danielle shook her head. 'Laurence, you're outrageous.'

'I hope you're not angry with me.'

Once again Danielle shook her head. 'No, no harm done. But I had to decline the offer.'

'It's a pity,' said Laurence. 'You'd've wiped the floor with the competition.'

As time passed Laurence and Danielle mingled with the other guests, most of whom Laurence seemed to know, and Danielle lost count of the people she was introduced to. Then they went into the dining room to get some food and wandered through the flat, drinking and chatting, until eventually they met up with Lilith and Dominic again.

Lilith grabbed Laurence and dragged him off to where Josh was standing and they were soon in deep conversation. When they returned, Lilith said to Danielle, 'I'm dying for a pee, and a chance to repair my make-up. Shall we find the ladies?'

'Good idea,' replied Danielle, who was beginning to feel the influence of the alcohol she'd been drinking. They left the men and went in search of the rest room.

Lilith led Danielle to one of the bedrooms, peeked inside and said, 'This'll do. It's empty.'

The bedroom was dimly lit, with just one lamp illuminating a double bed covered in a satin bedspread. In the wall opposite them, was an open door leading to an en-suite bathroom.

The two women entered the bedroom, and Lilith slipped the lock on the door. 'We don't want to be disturbed with our knickers down, do we?' she said. 'Come on Danielle, I'm bursting.'

The two of them went together into the bathroom and, with no trace of self-consciousness, Lilith hiked up the skirt of her dress to her waist, exposing the tops of her stockings, her suspender belt and the tiny black knickers she was wearing. She pulled her panties down, sat on the toilet and urinated noisily into the bowl.

Danielle couldn't help looking and saw the dark triangle of pubic hair between Lilith's legs as she sat on the toilet.

When she'd finished, Lilith dried herself, pulled up her knickers, adjusted her dress and said, 'Your turn,' as she rinsed her hands, opened her handbag, took out her make-up and squinted into the mirror over the hand-basin.

Danielle hesitated, then mentally shrugged. What the hell, she thought, and pulled up her skirt, lowered her panties and sat on the toilet and emptied her own bladder.

Lilith chatted away as if it were perfectly normal for two women to share a toilet together and Danielle assumed that where she came from, it was. When she'd finished she also dried herself, adjusted her clothing and joined Lilith at the mirror to patch up her make-up.

When they were satisfied with the results of their endeavours, and Lilith had sprayed a copious amount of perfume into her cleavage, they left the bathroom.

'What a lovely room,' said Lilith as she looked round.

'Isn't it,' agreed Danielle, and went to the window, pulled the curtain aside and looked at the view over the park outside. 'I bet this place is worth a fortune.'

'You could have one like it for yourself inside a year if you came and worked for me,' said Lilith, and came up closely behind Danielle.

'You really don't take no for an answer easily, do you?' said Danielle.

'No, I don't,' said the older woman, and slid her arms round Danielle's shoulders. 'Not ever.'

38

Danielle stiffened at the embrace, then relaxed. Her brain still clouded with alcohol. Lilith pushed herself against her and slid her hands down over the front of the younger woman's dress, cupping her breasts and lifting them slightly to feel their weight. Once satisfied, she ran her hands down over Danielle's belly into the V between her legs. Danielle moved her feet slightly apart to allow the older woman to slide one hand between them, into the secret place there. She could feel Lilith's breath hot and moist on her neck.

As they stood together, Danielle pushed against Lilith, moulding her breasts into her back. They were big and soft, yet at the same time very hard, and Danielle could feel the points of the other woman's nipples through the material of her dress and the thin bra beneath it.

Danielle had never been the object of another woman's desire before and the thought excited her tremendously. She turned her head and looked into Lilith's eyes, and they kissed lingeringly. Lilith's mouth was greasy with fresh lipstick and Danielle tasted it on her tongue. Now she knew what men tasted when they kissed a woman for the first time and she longed for more. She wanted them to make each other up, then smear each other's faces with hot, lustful kisses.

Danielle turned around and the two women embraced face to face. She ran her fingers down Lilith's back and felt the feminine curve of her buttocks and the outline of her suspender belt and panties under her dress. Suddenly Danielle desperately wanted to take Lilith's tight little knickers off, expose the wet cunt beneath them and explore it with her tongue.

Their kisses became wilder and they moved towards the bed. Danielle swallowed and said in a thick, breathy voice, 'I want to be naked with you.'

'So you shall, darling,' replied Lilith. 'Just have patience. We have all the time in the world. All night if you want.'

Right then, there was nothing Danielle wanted more and she told Lilith so, much to her delight.

They sat down together on the edge of the mattress and continued kissing. Danielle was lost in Lilith's hot, sweet mouth. It was totally different from kissing a man. Lilith's lips were soft and fat and her skin was smooth. Danielle rubbed her cheek against her new girlfriend's. She loved the feeling: no rough stubble, just a fine down, like mist on Lilith's skin.

The older woman ran her hand up Danielle's thigh, pushing her skirt up above her stocking tops to expose the bare, white flesh. 'Beautiful,' she breathed. 'You have beautiful legs. I was looking at them in the mirror before, when you were pissing.'

'Thank you,' said Danielle shyly, and she put her hand under Lilith's skirt into the heat between her thighs. She felt the double thickness of nylon at the top of Lilith's stockings, then the moist, soft bareness of her skin. Her knuckles touched the nylon of the panties that covered Lilith's pussy and she felt the hair beneath the material, warm and crinkly, damp and delightful.

Danielle's love tunnel began lubricating heavily as she felt Lilith's hair. All of a sudden, she felt her juices bubble between her legs with want for the other woman.

Lilith turned her back on Danielle and said, 'Unzip me.'

Danielle did as she was told, her fingers fumbling with the fastener, then pulling it down to Lilith's waist.

Danielle pushed the dress off Lilith's shoulders, exposing the black lacey bra that she was wearing beneath it. Lilith turned back to face her and Danielle looked down at the creamy orbs that filled the cups to bursting point.

'You're big,' she said, and put out her hand and touched the flesh through the black lace.

Lilith reached up behind her and undid the snaps at the back of her bra. She shrugged out of the straps, so that the garment dropped into her lap exposing her tits to Danielle's hungry eyes. The older woman's breasts were huge, with long, raspberry-red nipples, surrounded by dark aureoles as big as small saucers.

'I am, aren't I?' Lilith said. 'Do you like them?'

'Yes,' said Danielle, and she put her head down to Lilith's left tit and took the nipple in her mouth. She sucked at the gristle, smelling the perfume that Lilith had sprayed between her breasts in the bathroom. Lilith put her hand at the back of Danielle's head and held it close. Danielle sucked at the teat and as she did so, she could feel Lilith's heart beating in her ribcage like a trapped bird.

As she kissed and sucked at Lilith's tit, the older woman undid the hooks at the back of Danielle's dress and pulled it off her shoulders too, then undid the fastenings of Danielle's bra.

The two women separated and took off their dresses. Both were wearing black knickers, suspender belts and black stockings underneath, but there the similarity ended. Lilith was of a heavier build than Danielle, though her body was still firm, and her skin was darker.

They climbed on the bed together and began to caress each other's almost naked bodies. The satin bedspread underneath her felt cool, slippery and sensual on Danielle's bare skin, and once again she could feel her juice dribbling down through her pubic hair to soak the gusset of her knickers.

Lilith's mouth went down to Danielle's belly then, missing out her genital area, she began to kiss the bare skin of her thighs. Danielle almost cried out for Lilith to stop teasing her: to strip her damp knickers off, and expose the blonde fuzz between her slim legs. She wanted Lilith to put her dark head down to her pussy and attach the hot lips of her mouth to the hot lips of Danielle's hungry cunt that were weeping for the older woman's expert attentions, but she didn't dare ask. Instead she slid her mouth down the length of Lilith's body until they were side by side, in the sixty-nine position, and Danielle pulled Lilith's pants down to her knees, then tore them right off her body.

She hesitated then, as she looked at Lilith's cunt. She'd never been so close to a another woman's sex before. Lilith's pubic hair was thick and dark and a thin line of curls went up as far as her belly button. As Lilith scissored her legs to give Danielle a better view, she exuded a smell of female so dark and musky that Danielle almost swooned.

Danielle could feel Lilith's eyes on her as she moved closer to the opening to her vagina.

'You like?' asked Lilith.

'I love,' said Danielle, and she put out her tongue and touched it to the lips of Lilith's cunt that were dewed with a moisture so sweet, yet tart, that Danielle salivated at the taste. As her mouth covered Lilith's pussy, the older woman stiffened and reached down and grabbed two handfuls of Danielle's hair, forcing her blonde head hard against her own quim.

Lilith's pubic hair was like fine wire on Danielle's face, and as she plastered her mouth against the slit it opened like a spring flower under her lips and the taste of Lilith's juices became even stronger. Danielle licked around the opening, then poked her tongue inside and found Lilith's clitoris in its protective membrane. It was hard and erect under her tongue and as she began to tease it with the tip, Lilith cried out with pleasure.

Lilith let go of her hair and Danielle came up for a breath of air, as she felt her own knickers being pulled off her hips and pushed down her legs and over the end of her feet. As her own pussy was exposed to Lilith's eyes she opened her legs and allowed her lover easy access to her vulva.

She felt Lilith's head go down and her wet mouth join with her own wet puss. As Lilith's tongue entered her passage, the most marvellous feeling of wellbeing, mixed with an almost unbearable excitement ran through the length of Danielle's body, from the tips of her toes to the end of each individual hair on her head.

She closed her legs gently on Lilith's head, to trap her face against her cunt, and she put her own face down on the dark damp fragrant hair between Lilith's legs once more.

In tandem the two women licked, sucked, kissed, nibbled,

nuzzled and snogged each other's private parts, whilst their hands ran over each other's bodies, finding and exciting their erogenous zones as they went, until finally Danielle could stand it no longer. She felt an orgasm growing inside her like a balloon being blown up, until the pressure was too much and it burst through her body in an explosion of joy.

As if she was only waiting for the novice lesbian to come, Lilith followed suit a few seconds later. Danielle felt her begin to buck and heave against her mouth and had her first experience of another woman's frenzied climax at first hand.

They lay back together on the damp bedspread and pulled themselves round to lay in a sweaty embrace together. Their faces were coated with the slime from the other's pussy and gently they licked each other clean.

'That was wonderful,' said Danielle. 'I had no idea.'

'We haven't even started yet,' said Lilith. 'There are delights in store for you that you never dreamed existed.'

'I can't wait,' said Danielle.

39

When Danielle and Lilith were dressed again and had repaired their make-up, they exchanged a brief kiss before returning to the party. Laurence was waiting for them, leaning against the wall of the bar, with a drink in hand.

'Had fun girls?' he asked.

Danielle looked at Lilith. Now what? she thought.

'We've just had a tinkle,' said Lilith.

'Rather a long tinkle, I would have thought,' retorted Laurence.

'It's none of your business,' said Lilith, and wrinkled her nose at him. 'What does a mere man know anyway, eh Danielle?'

'What indeed?' Danielle agreed.

'Now are you going to get us some more drinks, or do we have to fetch our own?' said Lilith to Laurence.

'I'll get them,' said Laurence, who placed his glass on a small table close to where they were standing and went off to the bar.

When he returned, he said, 'Do you want to go soon Danielle? I've done all I need to do here.'

'What an ardent suitor you are Laurence,' said Lilith. 'You're almost bowling the girl over with your enthusiasm to get her alone.'

Laurence smiled. 'Danielle and I have an understanding,' he said. 'Don't we Danielle?'

Danielle nodded.

In fact she didn't mind leaving at all. The drinks had gone to her head, the place was very noisy and she could do with some peace.

'I'm ready when you are, Laurence,' she said. 'I could use some fresh air. Could you get my coat?'

Laurence nodded and left the bar in search of the cloakroom. When he'd gone, Lilith said, 'Now be sure to call me soon Danielle. I'd love to see you again. Like I said, we didn't even start on the possibilities that we could explore together in there tonight.'

Danielle nodded. 'You can count on it,' she said.

At that moment Laurence came back into the room carrying Danielle's coat over his arm. He helped her into it and they both embraced Lilith before they made their way back to lift and down into the street to Laurence's car.

'What were you really up to with Lilith?' he asked when they were driving down Park Lane.

'We had a fuck,' said Danielle. 'If that's what two women do.'

'I knew it,' said Laurence. 'Lilith had that look, from the moment she laid eyes on you.'

'Did she?' said Danielle, looking over at him.

Laurence nodded. 'Yes. I knew she'd try and get you into bed.'

'She succeeded,' said Danielle.

'Was it good?'

'Not bad.'

'So, are you thinking of converting?'

'To what?'

'To being a sister of Lesbos?'

'I don't know about that.'

'I hope not. You're too sexy to lose to a bunch of dykes. But even if you were, I've got a cure.'

'What's that?'

'A good fuck from someone with a prick between his legs. A prick that desires a real woman.'

Even though she was tired, Danielle found herself responding to Laurence's words. 'Is that right?' she said.

'That's right. A feminine woman who wants to be filled with the spunk of her man.'

'How filled?'

'To the brim.'

'Sounds interesting. Can't you drive a little faster?'

With a smile, Laurence put his foot on the accelerator.

When they got back to his flat, he poured out two brandies and gave one to Danielle. She accepted it and collapsed onto the sofa. 'I'm bushed,' she said.

'Not too bushed for a bit of fun, I hope.'

'It depends. You'll have to convince me.'

'I don't think I'll have any trouble there,' he replied. 'I know how to turn you on.'

Danielle smiled.

Laurence went and sat next to her, took her glass out of her hand, put it on the table next to the sofa and took her in his arms. They kissed: gently at first, then more deeply, and finally – as Laurence's hand found Danielle's breast – passionately.

She moaned in the back of her throat and they broke apart. Laurence said, 'Did you enjoy making love to a woman?'

Danielle nodded. 'It was different,' she said.

'You've never done it before?'

She shook her head. 'Never.'

'Do you fancy a replay?'

Danielle nodded again, and blushed.

'I believe Lilith has some interesting toys at her disposal,' he said.

'Does she?'

'So I've heard.'

'What kind of toys?'

'Strap on dildos. Vibrators.'

Danielle squirmed at the thought. She felt herself getting wet and flexed the muscles of her cunt. 'Sounds good,' she said.

'You're a disgusting woman.'

'Do you think so?'

Laurence nodded and kissed her again.

I wonder why, she thought as their lips met.

Laurence's hand found her breast again and tweaked the hard nipple through her clothes. Danielle's tits felt tender and bruised and she cried out in pain. At the sound, Laurence tweaked the other nipple even harder.

'That hurts,' Danielle protested.

'You've been a naughty girl, you deserve some punishment that hurts.'

'No,' said Danielle, but Laurence stood up, grabbed her hand and dragged her off to the bedroom where he threw her roughly onto the bed. He ripped her dress off her shoulders, down over her body, and threw it across the room.

Danielle covered her breasts with her crossed arms. She'd seen Laurence like this before, after she'd fucked

Charlie in front of him, and it scared her, although it also turned her on. But this time he seemed even angrier.

He went over to the wardrobe, opened it, and fumbled around inside. When he turned to face her again he was holding a bunch of leather straps with silver buckles at one end of each.

'What are you doing?' she asked.

'You'll see. Roll over.'

'Laurence . . .'

'*Do it.*'

The tone of his voice made her obey without question. She turned over onto her front and he came over to the bed and began to fasten her wrists to the bed head with the straps. He tightened them cruelly, until she was afraid her circulation would be cut off.

When her hands were securely bound, he went back to the wardrobe and brought out a scarf which he used to gag Danielle.

On his final visit, he emerged holding a vicious looking bull whip with red silk plaited into the end.

Danielle was really terrified by now and she was afraid she was going to piss herself.

What have I got into this time, she thought, as she pulled at the straps that shackled her to the bed.

Laurence took off his jacket and shirt and stood bare chested beside the bed with the whip in his hand. He cracked it over Danielle's body and at the sound she cringed on the mattress. Although she was terrified at what was about to happen, her cunt was betraying her. It was sopping wet with desire for the man and she could feel it open as she lay there looking over her shoulder at Laurence.

Then he laid the lash across her buttocks. Although the

touch was light across the thin material of her panties, the pain she felt was sharp and brought tears to Danielle's eyes, and even more lubrication from her love canal.

She grunted into the gag that was fastened round her mouth and shook her head. She wanted Laurence to stop, but at the same time she wanted him to beat her hard, until her blood and pussy juice mixed between her legs.

Laurence laid the thong once more over her bottom, a little lower the second time, so that the leather bit into the tops of her thighs.

Danielle stiffened at the pain and Laurence snapped the whip across her buttocks once more. It still hurt, but in a different, more pleasing way. The fourth stroke was even more pleasant, like a kiss, and the cheeks of her arse began to feel warm under her knickers.

As Laurence laid the plaited leather across her bottom again, Danielle pushed her mound of venus into the mattress and stimulated her clitoris against it, through the thin, wet silk of her panties.

Again and again Laurence whipped her, a little harder each time, and each time Danielle loved the feeling more.

She looked up at Laurence from where she was lying and saw the sweat running down his bare torso, the look of concentration on his face, and heard his breath hissing between bared teeth.

As he beat her on it, her bottom was a soaking swamp of sexual need. Her juices squeezed out through the slit of her cunt and all she could think of was her desire to be shagged by the man who was giving her such delicious pain.

As if he could read her mind, Laurence dropped the whip, tore off his trousers, shoes, socks and underpants to expose his knob rearing out of his thatch of pubic hair, upright, red and angry. He ripped Danielle's panties from her hips, snapping the elastic around her waist as he did so. Then he lifted her arse into the air and mounted her from behind, forcing his cock into her cunt like an animal. Not that much forcing was necessary, as she was as open and ready as she'd ever been in her life. She felt his tool slide up inside her with one smooth, wonderful shove, and Laurence began to batter at her arse with his groin. Danielle came almost immediately, then had a second orgasm, and a third on top of it, as he rammed his body at her. She was in heaven and pushed her arse back against his cock. His breath was whistling out of his lungs as he slammed at her harder and harder, cursing her as he shagged her beautifully, defenceless body, until finally, with roar like a wounded animal he let go a mighty spurt of spunk into her waiting womb.

40

Laurence pulled out of Danielle and collapsed onto the bed next to her. He was breathing hard after his exertions and he lay there for a minute, before reaching up and pulling down the gag in her mouth. 'Did you like that?' he asked.

She worked spit into her dry mouth and replied, 'It was good.'

'Better than being played with by a woman?'

'Different.'

He slapped her bottom hard, then laughed and moved up the bed and unfastened the straps that bound her to the bedstead. Danielle massaged the blood back into her hands, rolled off the bed and went into the bathroom where she took a piss with the door open, knowing that Laurence could see her from where he was lying. Her desire for more sex was blatant and she knew that he knew it. She felt insatiable. She wiped herself on a handful of soft toilet paper, then walked back into the bedroom and stood by the bed. She knew he was looking at the sticky blonde hairs between her legs, matted together so that they hardly hid the entrance to her vagina.

As she stood there, she could see the effect she was having on Laurence. His cock rolled across his thigh as it hardened, then rose and pointed in the direction of her pussy.

'More?' she asked.

'Suck me,' he ordered.

She did as he said, kneeling beside the bed and taking his semi-erect penis between her lips and suckling it like a baby at the breast, until it became properly hard. She massaged his organ with her mouth, rolling the knob of it round the insides of her cheeks and up the back of her throat. She teased the hole with the tip of her tongue whilst she played with his balls with her fingers, until she felt the first stirrings of another orgasm in his scrotum. She fellated him harder, willing him to come with her eyes, which she fastened on his as she worked on him. As she looked, his knob moved in her mouth and she felt the spunk shoot up the length of it and splash her throat. She sucked every last drop up and swallowed it greedily, loving the salty, slightly ammoniac taste of it. Then she laid her head on his stomach and watched as his knob shrank back down, whilst Laurence stroked her hair.

After a few minutes she climbed back onto the bed. 'It's your turn,' she said. 'Make me come with your mouth.'

He slid down the length of her and she opened her legs and he put his head between them. She could feel him examining her cunt and he opened the lips of it with two fingers before gently placing his tongue into her centre.

She shivered as she felt the hot organ exploring the inner lips of her labia. He found her clitoris and ran the very tip of his tongue around its hardness. He was very gentle, but she wanted roughness and pushed his head closer to her cunt. He guessed her need and sucked a mouthful of flesh up into his mouth and chewed on it. She cried out and beat her fists onto the mattress beneath her. Laurence chewed harder and she thought of Lilith's mouth where his was. She pushed her hips upwards and felt her soft flesh against the hardness of his teeth. Her whole world became centred on her pussy and like a huge dark flower opening between her legs she orgasmed with a scream.

Laurence crawled back up the bed and they lay together without saying a word. Within a few minutes Danielle fell asleep.

She woke at nine on Sunday morning. During the night Laurence had pulled the bed covers over them. She looked over at him. He was still asleep. She got up without waking him and dressed. Then she scribbled a hasty note, saying she'd call him soon, before going back to her car and driving home.

When she arrived, she had a bath and slipped into a shirt and jeans before going out once more to get the papers. Then she tidied the already spotless house before Nigel got home.

He arrived at about three. They kissed perfunctorily and Danielle poured him a drink whilst he changed. When he was sitting comfortably on the sofa in the living room, she said, 'Did you have a good weekend?'

'Not bad. How was yours?'

She shrugged. 'It was OK.'

'I called you last night, there was no answer.'

'I went to bed early.' For some reason she wanted him to believe her.

He smiled nastily. 'Alone?' he asked.

She was getting bored with him. 'Of course,' she lied.

He obviously didn't believe her. And why should he? she thought.

'If you say so,' he said.

'Would you care?'

He shrugged. 'Did you see Richard at all?'

She shook her head.

'We must ask him round again soon.'

'If you want.' She wasn't interested in Richard.

'I spoke to Sir George last night. He was at the conference. He was full of praise for you.'

'That's nice.'

'He can't wait to see you again, he said.'

'Good. Did he mention your promotion?'

'Not in so many words, but he wants a long chat at the weekend.'

'Good,' she said again.

'So make sure you take all your sexiest clothes. I want the old boy slavering after you.'

'I will,' she said. But she wasn't that interested in Sir George either.

They went to bed early but didn't make love. Danielle sensed that Nigel wouldn't touch her all week, so that she'd be especially horny when she met Sir George again. She felt like a lamb being offered as a sacrifice.

The next few days passed slowly for Danielle. She felt disorientated and strange. Nigel was paying her little attention and she knew why.

On Wednesday morning she phoned Lilith.

She got through to a receptionist who took her name, then put her on hold.

The next voice she heard was Lilith's. 'Danielle, darling,'

she screeched. 'I'm so glad you called. How are you?'

'Fine,' replied Danielle. 'How are you?'

'All the better for hearing your voice. When are we going to get together?'

'Whenever,' replied Danielle. 'How about tomorrow.'

'Let me check my diary. Are you free for lunch?'

'Yes,' said Danielle.

'So am I. Why don't you come here? We can eat upstairs in my flat. It's so much more cosy than a restaurant. I'll get my secretary to organise some food. What do you say?'

'Sounds lovely,' said Danielle, and she felt that old familiar itch in her belly. The itch that only sexual gratification could scratch.

'One o'clock then. At the address on the card I gave you.'

'I'll be there,' said Danielle and hung up the phone.

The next day Danielle paid particular attention to her appearance as she got ready to go out. She bathed and washed her hair and after she dried it, she brushed it to a golden cascade around her neck and shoulders. She made up her face carefully, once again paying special attention to her eyes, and coating a thick, glossy layer of lipstick onto her mouth. She decided that she'd wear scarlet underwear to meet Lilith. Scarlet. The colour of sin. She had a brand new silk set that she'd never worn, which she had been saving for a special occasion. She carefully unpacked the delicate garments from their cellophane wrapper. The bra was unstructured and could barely contain the fullness of her breasts. The knickers were tiny and the gusset slid into the crack of her cunt as soon as she put them on. Her pussy immediately began to produce a stream of liquid. The suspender belt was no more than four thin straps of silk attached to an elasticated strap that hung low on her hips. The effect was stunning and turned Danielle on even more as she looked at herself in the mirror. She found a new pair of black nylons which she rolled up her legs and fastened tightly to the clips at the end of the suspenders. Over her undies she put on a red dress, with a tight, low-cut bodice and a short pencil skirt. Finally she found a pair of scarlet high-heeled shoes with very pointed toes which took her height to over six feet. She felt like an amazon as she twisted and turned in front of the mirror to get the full effect of the outfit. Over the top she wore her Burberry mac with the collar up, filled a red leather handbag with her make-up, address book and other bits and pieces, and left the house just after twelve. She drove up to Soho where Lilith's office/flat was located and left the Golf in an NCP car park before making the short walk to her destination.

Danielle found the building she was seeking easily. It was in a sixties development at the back of Wardour Street. She went to the office first. She was slightly early for her appointment. The receptionist told her that Lilith was just winding up a meeting and asked if Danielle would care to take a seat. She cared, and sat on a long leather sofa with a glass coffee table covered in magazines in front of it. She picked up a copy of that month's *Elle* which she flicked through without taking in a word. She was in a high state of sexual excitement and could feel the dampness between her thighs and could almost hear the slurping sound that her cunt made each time she moved her legs. But at the same time, she was shy about seeing Lilith again and wondered if she should have come.

At one o'clock precisely Lilith came through a door that led into the inner sanctum of the office, with a tall, good-looking man of about thirty in tow. She smiled at Danielle when she saw her, shook the man's hand briskly and bade him farewell. Then she watched as he left the reception area, before turning to Danielle, taking hold of both her hands, tugging her to her feet and giving her a kiss on each cheek.

'Danielle,' she cried. 'I'm so glad you could make it. Come upstairs. The martinis are ready and my faithful secretary has been to Fortnum's to get us lunch. I don't know about you but I'm starving. Making money always gives me an appetite. And with that stud you just saw, I'm going to make a mint.'

Lilith was dressed in a black suit over a white blouse, dark nylons, and high-heeled black court shoes. Her hair was up in a French pleat and she wore a pair of severe, black-rimmed glasses. She looked every inch the successful businesswoman and Danielle found it hard to imagine that she had made passionate love to her just a few days before.

'Hello,' she replied, and returned the kisses.

Lilith said to the receptionist. 'I'll be upstairs for a couple of hours having lunch. Hold all calls.' Then she turned to Danielle. 'This way,' she said, and led her through another door and up two flights of stairs to her flat.

It was very small and furnished in leather and chrome with white Venetian blinds at the windows. In the centre of the room a table had been set for two and a selection of cold food was laid out on the sideboard next to a cooler that held two bottles of champagne, beside a jug of clear liquid which Danielle took to be the martinis. She was right. Lilith made straight for the jug and poured out two generous glasses. 'Olive or lemon?' she asked.

'Lemon,' replied Danielle, and Lilith popped a twist into one of the glasses and passed it to her, before dropping a stuffed olive into her own.

'I'll remember next time,' she said.

The martini was almost pure gin, and Danielle felt its strength as she took a sip. 'You'll get me drunk,' she said.

'That's the idea,' replied Lilith. 'It'll help you relax.'

Danielle smiled in return.

'Take off your coat, dear,' said Lilith. 'It looks as if you're not staying.'

Up until then Danielle hadn't been sure that she was, but at Lilith's words, she put her glass on the table, took off her mac and draped it over the back of a leather armchair.

'That dress is sensational,' said Lilith. 'You shouldn't hide your light under a bushel. I feel like an old frump next to you.'

'You look great,' said Danielle, and picked up her glass and took another sip.

'So what have you been up to?' asked Lilith.

'Nothing much. Just the usual dull routine of an everyday housewife.'

'We'll have to change all that,' Lilith replied with a lascivious wink. 'Now what will you have to eat?'

The meal was delicious and the champagne that Lilith opened to drink with it – combined with the martini that Danielle had drunk before lunch – soon mellowed her mood. By the time they'd eaten, and a pot of coffee was bubbling over a spirit stove, and Lilith was opening a bottle of thirty-year-old brandy, the two women were chatting like old friends.

When the coffee was ready, Lilith pulled the blinds down over the window and she and Danielle took their cups and brandy glasses to a leather sofa with a glass coffee table in front of it – the twins of the ones in the reception downstairs – and sat next to each other.

Danielle knew what was coming next. She could feel herself shaking at the sexual tension in the room and gulped down a mouthful of fiery liquor.

The room was dim and warm with the blinds drawn, and Danielle watched as Lilith took off her glasses and reached up and undid her hair, letting it fall about her shoulders.

'That's better,' she said. She put her cup and glass on the coffee table, took Danielle's from her and placed them next to her own, then leaned over and kissed Danielle full on the mouth.

Danielle responded to the kiss hungrily. Although Lilith's lipstick had been rubbed off her mouth as she ate, Danielle could still taste the remnants of it and it reminded her of their previous love session. She sucked at Lilith's lips eagerly.

The older woman placed her left hand on Danielle's right breast and her nipple immediately responded to the delicate touch. 'Shall we go into the bedroom?' said Lilith.

Their drinks forgotten, they both rose, and Lilith took Danielle's hand, leading her through a door into the bedroom.

It too was in twilight, with another set of venetian blinds pulled down over the window. The bed was vast and covered in a black silk cover. At the foot of it stood a huge TV set with a video hooked up to it. Lilith went over to the bed and threw back the silk coverlet and the thin duvet beneath to expose black silk sheets.

The two women embraced. In their heels, they were almost the same height. They kissed again and Danielle felt the room spin as Lilith's lips attached to hers like suckers.

'Turn around, darling,' said Lilith.

Danielle did so and Lilith pulled down the zip at the back of her dress, which Danielle pushed down over her hips and allowed to drop to the floor. She stepped out of it before turning to face Lilith again.

'I love your undies,' said Lilith. 'The colour suits you perfectly. Let me show you mine.'

The dark-haired woman took off the jacket to her suit and threw it across the room. Then she unzipped her skirt and dropped it to the carpet. Her shirt came off next exposing brief white underwear. Lacy bra and knickers and a white suspender belt.

'Very virginal,' she said. 'What do you think?'

'You look lovely,' said Danielle.

Lilith took Danielle's hand and led her to the bed. When Danielle started to take off her shoes, Lilith stopped her. 'Leave them on,' she said. 'I love the smell of leather. I want to dress us both in leather one day and make love to you fully clothed.'

Danielle remembered the whipping that Laurence had given her – the feel of the leather thongs that had bound her and the feel of the leather whip on her backside – and her cunt seemed to open as Lilith spoke. As if she knew, the older woman put her hand between Danielle's legs and pushed the wet silk against her hair. 'You're soaking, darling,' she whispered.

'You turn me on,' replied Danielle.

Lilith eased Danielle's wet knickers off and put her head down to the blonde fur between the girl's thighs. Danielle opened her legs wide. Lilith put her hand onto her cunt and gently parted the lips, then kissed Danielle's pussy. Danielle felt liquid fire in her womb as Lilith's black hair spread across her naked belly and thighs and the older woman's mouth moved lovingly on her sex.

Danielle put her hand down and gathered a handful of Lilith's hair, which she rubbed gently through her fingers. It felt like silk to her touch. Lilith's tongue probed at Danielle's tunnel of love as the girl played with her hair, and she opened her legs wider still, so that Lilith could push more of her face into the hot, dark, wet cavern between her legs.

Lilith kissed and nuzzled Danielle's pussy for what seemed like an age and each lick and suck was heaven. When, eventually, she moved her head to look up at Danielle, her face was covered in slick, silver juice which caught in Lilith's hair as it flopped forward. They both moved so that they could kiss again and Danielle licked her own slime off Lilith's face like a mother animal cleaning its baby after birth. Her own liquid tasted wonderful in her mouth and between licks they kissed hard.

'Now do me,' said Lilith. 'Immerse yourself in my wetness.'

Without a second thought Danielle went down to Lilith's pussy. She pulled the white panties she was wearing over her hips, down her legs and off. Then she put her face close to the hot swamp between Lilith's legs.

Her smell was overpowering. It was rich and dark and sensual. Although she'd smelt it once before, it was still mysterious and intriguing to Danielle. She pushed Lilith's wiry pubic hair apart with two fingers and studied the wet folds of skin at the entrance to her vagina. Her cunt lips were red and swollen and inside was pink and coated with grey viscous juice. Danielle found Lilith's clitoris and she bent down and touched it with the tip of her tongue, making Lilith jump at the sensation, as if she'd been given a slight electric shock. Danielle heard the older woman moan as she explored deeper into her pussy with her mouth.

Lilith reached for Danielle and pulled her round so that Danielle could carry on exploring her cunt and put her nose into the crack of Lilith's arse. Lilith put her fingers into Danielle's cunt. First one, then two, then three, and as Danielle's tunnel opened, four and then finally her thumb. Danielle had never been fist-fucked before and the experience was magical. Lilith forced her whole hand up into Danielle's womb and opened it wide. The young blonde stopped sucking at Lilith's cunt and looked over her shoulder and the older woman blew her a kiss. Danielle's whole being was on fire from the sensation of Lilith's hand opening and closing deep inside her, and she came with a sob.

Delicately, Lilith removed her hand from Danielle's orifice. They moved up together to be head to head once more and embraced.

'That was marvellous,' said Danielle. 'No one's ever done that to me before.'

'I've got small hands,' said Lilith. 'It's easy.'

'It's wonderful,' breathed Danielle, and leaned over and kissed her lesbian lover again. The kiss deepened and Danielle put her hand on Lilith's breast, then slid it down, over her belly and between her legs. She wanted to make Lilith come and repay the favour she'd done Danielle. Her fingers found Lilith's clitoris again and she teased it with her nails. Lilith stiffened at the touch, and as Danielle ran her fingers round the blood filled organ, Lilith relaxed into her arms and orgasmed as they kissed.

They parted and lay back on the bed. Danielle closed her eyes. She felt Lilith climb off the mattress and heard the sound of her feet padding into the next room. Then she heard voices – Lilith's and that of a familiar male. Danielle opened her eyes and saw Lilith and Laurence standing in the doorway. Laurence was holding a video cassette in one hand. Surprised at his appearance, Danielle pulled the cover up to hide her naked pussy.

'Laurence. Where did you come from? How did you get in here?'

'I've got my own key. I've been here for twenty minutes.' Danielle pulled the bed cover higher to hide her breasts, even though she was still wearing her bra. 'Shy?' asked Laurence. 'You weren't so shy the other night,' and he held up the video.

'What?' said Danielle, mystified.

Laurence grinned nastily, walked over to the TV set, switched it on and put the video into the slot in the VCR. He pressed a button and snow appeared on the screen. Then it cleared in a flurry of horizontal lines and Danielle saw herself and Lilith in the bedroom at the penthouse where the party had been held on Saturday night. They were standing by the bed in each other's arms, kissing, and Danielle saw herself rubbing Lilith's bottom thorough her dress. They moved towards the bed and Danielle heard herself through the speakers on the TV, say 'I want to be naked with you'. The film ran on and Danielle witnessed the lovemaking she had shared with Lilith that night. She couldn't believe it. As Danielle watched, Lilith collected her clothes and got dressed.

The video ended as Danielle and Lilith got off the bed and began to get dressed. Laurence turned off the TV and retrieved the cassette from the VCR.

'Lilith made you an offer the other night and you declined it,' he said 'A very good offer . . . Lilith?'

Lilith, who by then was fully dressed, nodded her head.

'As the person who introduced you, I would have made a tidy sum myself,' Laurence continued. 'I know you've got the talent and disposition for the job. So I want you to reconsider.'

Danielle lay on the bed and looked from Lilith to Laurence and back. She'd been betrayed. And so easily.

She shook her head. 'No,' she said.

'Why not?'

'I don't do it for money.'

'Yes you do,' said Laurence. 'Charlie . . . Remember him? He paid me three hundred quid to screw you the other night.'

'You bastard,' said Danielle. 'You slimy bastard.'

Laurence shrugged. 'So I know you can do it. All that we have to find is the price.'

Danielle shook her head again.

Laurence held up the cassette. 'Then I'm afraid I'll have to send this to Sir George Guggenheim. Your husband's boss. I know he's not exactly a pillar of morality himself. But I also know that the sight of one of his executives' wives in bed with another woman, although it might turn him on, would bode ill for that executive. Especially one coming up for a promotion.'

'How do you know that?' choked Danielle through pale

272

lips. She felt nauseous and suddenly all alone in a hostile world.

'I make it my business to know *everything*,' said Laurence.

'You bastard,' said Danielle again, then looked at Lilith. 'And you're a bitch.'

'But a *nice* bitch,' said Lilith. 'Come on Danielle. This is just a hiccup. Come and work with me. You'll make a mint with your talent for sex. *And* we can still do what we did today. I know you loved it.'

'I wouldn't touch either of you again if you paid me,' said Danielle, and both Laurence and Lilith laughed cruelly.

Laurence handed the cassette to Lilith and began to get undressed. 'Oh no,' he said. 'Watching that's got me horny. I'm going to fuck you Danielle.'

'No,' she protested, and shrank even further back onto the bed.

'Yes,' said Laurence, as he took off the last of his clothes and stood naked in front of her with his cock erect. 'Fight me if you want, Danielle. It'll make it all the sweeter to have you.'

He walked over to the bed and dragged the bed cover out of Danielle's hands, pulled it away so that he could see her, and tossed it on to the floor. He looked down at her, dressed only in her scarlet bra, suspender belt, nylons and shoes, and grinned again. He could see the wetness in her pubic hair from when she'd orgasmed with Lilith, and Danielle could feel it, and much as she wished herself dry, she couldn't be.

But then, she thought. If I were dry, it would only hurt me more.

She covered herself with both hands, but Laurence

knocked them away, then pulled her legs apart. She wanted to fight him but she knew it would be useless. He was much stronger than she was and it would be a pointless gesture. Better to get it over and done with.

Laurence climbed onto the bed next to her and kissed her roughly, forcing his tongue into her mouth. She knew that he wanted her to struggle, but instead she lay slackly in his embrace.

Angrily he grabbed her tits and massaged them hard, but she didn't respond, just lay trembling with anger under his hands. He rolled on top of her and pushed the helmet of his knob against the lips of her pussy. Her cunt was open and accepted him easily. He forced himself inside, trying to hurt her, but she was too well lubricated. He began to screw her furiously, pumping hard at her quim until, despite herself, Danielle began to respond with answering strokes of her own. But even as she did so, she felt tears well up in her eyes and roll down her cheeks.

He pushed himself up on his hands and looked down at her tear-stained face with a cruel smile, then shortened his strokes until his balls emptied into her. Over his shoulder Danielle could see Lilith watching Laurence rape her. She turned her head away as she felt the jet of juice from his scrotum fill her womb.

He pulled roughly out of her, got off the bed and began to dress again. When he was finished he said, 'Come on Lilith. Let's leave our shrinking violet to get dressed and think about what she's going to do.'

Laurence and Lilith went back into the living room and closed the door behind them. Trembling still, Danielle got out of bed and hastily dressed herself. She dried her tears, then wiped her sopping cunt on the black bedcover and left the white stains for Lilith's laundry to deal with. When she was ready she went and joined them.

They were sitting opposite each other, drinking brandy. Danielle had never felt such hate for anyone as she felt then. 'If I agree to what you want me to do,' she said. 'Will you give me the tape?'

'In time,' said Laurence. 'When you've earned your keep.'

Which meant never, thought Danielle. Bastards. And even if they did give it to her, that didn't mean they hadn't made copies.

One day I'll get even, she vowed.

'Very well,' she said. 'You win. I'll do it.'

Laurence and Lilith smiled triumphantly at each other.

'Phone me tomorrow night,' said Lilith. 'I'll have your first assignment. I promise you'll never regret it.'

'Very well,' said Danielle. She picked up her handbag, then turned and left them without a backward glance.

41

Danielle collected her car from the car park and drove home. When she arrived, it wasn't yet four and she poured herself a drink and sat in the living room. She felt dirty and used by what had happened at Lilith's flat and vowed that it would never happen again, no matter what she had said to Laurence.

So, she thought. This is what my life has come to. My husband, who promised to love and honour me, wants to watch me fuck our next-door neighbour. And when I'm not doing that, he's quite happy that I should screw his boss, so that he can get the promotion he wants.

And as for my boyfriend. He's a nasty little pimp who wants to blackmail me into allowing myself to be rented out to a lesbian who, between taking me to bed herself, wants to sell me to dirty old men to service.

This is as low as I can sink, she realised. Everyone I've trusted has let me down and I want out. As far away as possible, where no one knows me. But where can I go?

She sat and drank and considered her position. Suddenly she had a brainwave and smiled. Of course. Why didn't I think of it before? There's only one place where I can hide away and no one will ever think of looking for me. One place where I can get a fresh start, away from all this.

Where they said I'd always be welcome. And her smile broadened.

The next morning she watched Nigel leave for work as usual and gave him no indication that it would be the last time.

When he was safely out of the way, Danielle dressed in black Levis, a blue chambray shirt, black boots and a leather jacket. She packed a small bag with the bare necessities and called a cab. She didn't want the car that Nigel had given her, much as she loved it. A fresh start, she thought. No hangovers from the past. Just what I stand up in, some clean knickers, and my make-up bag. That's the spirit, she thought.

When the cab arrived, she told the driver to take her to Waterloo Station.

'Going on your holidays, love?' he asked.

'You could say that,' she replied. She turned her head to discourage further conversation and watched the familiar streets roll by the windows of the car as it headed towards the centre of London. She wondered when and if she'd ever see them again.

At the station she bought a single ticket to Drenham and went to the departures board to find out which train to catch. There was only one. It left on the hour and stopped at every tiny station en route. Danielle didn't care. She had all the time in the world.

She got a coffee from a stall and watched as the people bustled around her. All of them with somewhere to go, she thought. Except me.

But she did have somewhere to go and resolved in future not to feel so sorry for herself. She got on the train and found a corner seat in the front carriage. It was almost deserted as it started its slow journey in the direction of the south coast.

The train finally pulled into Drenham station at twelve-fifteen. Danielle was the only passenger to alight. She carried her bag to the front of the station, where a lone porter stood leaning on a broom.

'Are there any taxis around here?' she asked.

He pulled a face. 'Shouldn't think so. Not at this time. Maybe later, when the rush starts.'

She looked around the deserted forecourt. 'There's a rush here?'

He grinned. 'Not much of one, I'll admit. Not like in London. Where you going?'

'Do the Harveys still run their garage here?'

'Dave and Johnny? Sure.'

'Is it far?' she asked.

'Nothing's far round here. Go up the road, turn right and the garage is about a mile down on your left. Can't miss it. You related?'

'Not yet. But who knows?'

'You'll have to be some kind of woman to tie one of them two down,' said the porter. 'There's a lot round here tried. And failed.'

'Oh, I'm some kind of woman all right,' said Danielle, and she picked up her suitcase and started to walk towards her new life.

Headline Delta Erotic Survey

In order to provide the kind of books you like to read – and to
qualify for a free erotic novel of the Editor's choice – we
would appreciate it if you would complete the following
survey and send your answers, together with any further
comments, to:

> Headline Book Publishing
> FREEPOST (WD 4984)
> London
> NW1 0YR

1. Are you male or female?
2. Age? Under 20 / 20 to 30 / 30 to 40 / 40 to 50 /
    50 to 60 / 60 to 70 / over
3. At what age did you leave full-time education?
4. Where do you live? (Main geographical area)
5. Are you a regular erotic book buyer / a regular book
    buyer in general / both?
6. How much approximately do you spend a year on erotic
    books / on books in general?
7. How did you come by this book?
7a. If you bought it, did you purchase from:
    a national bookchain / a high street store / a newsagent /
    a motorway station / an airport / a railway station /
    other . . .
8. Do you find erotic books easy / hard to come by?
8a. Do you find Headline Delta erotic books easy / hard
    to come by?
9. Which are the best / worst erotic books you have ever
    read?
9a. Which are the best / worst Headline Delta erotic books
    you have ever read?
10. Within the erotic genre there are many periods,
    subjects and literary styles. Which of the following
    do you prefer:
10a. (period) historical / Victorian / C20th /contemporary /
    future?
10b. (subject) nuns / whores & whorehouses /
    Continental frolics / s&m / vampires / modern realism /
    escapist fantasy / science fiction?

10c. (styles) hardboiled / humorous / hardcore / ironic / romantic / realistic?

10d. Are there any other ingredients that particularly appeal to you?

11. We try to create a cover appearance that is suitable for each title. Do you consider them to be successful?

12. Would you prefer them to be less explicit / more explicit?

13. We would be interested to hear of your other reading habits. What other types of books do you read?

14. Who are your favourite authors?

15. Which newspapers do you read?

16. Which magazines?

17 Do you have any other comments or suggestions to make?

A selection of Erotica from Headline

FAIR LADIES OF PEACHAM PLACE	Beryl Ambridge	£5.99 ☐
EROTICON HEAT	Anonymous	£5.99 ☐
SCANDALOUS LIAISONS	Anonymous	£5.99 ☐
FOUR PLAY	Felice Ash	£5.99 ☐
THE TRIAL	Samantha Austen	£5.99 ☐
NAKED INTENT	Becky Bell	£5.99 ☐
VIXENS OF NIGHT	Valentina Cilescu	£5.99 ☐
NEW TERM AT LECHLADE COLLEGE	Lucy Cunningham-Brown	£5.99 ☐
THE PLEASURE RING	Kit Gerrard	£5.99 ☐
SPORTING GIRLS	Faye Rossignol	£5.99 ☐

All Headline books are available at your local bookshop or newsagent, or can be ordered direct from the publisher. Just tick the titles you want and fill in the form below. Prices and availability subject to change without notice.

Headline Book Publishing, Cash Sales Department, Bookpoint, 39 Milton Park, Abingdon, OXON, OX14 4TD, UK. If you have a credit card you may order by telephone – 01235 400400.

Please enclose a cheque or postal order made payable to Bookpoint Ltd to the value of the cover price and allow the following for postage and packing:

UK & BFPO: £1.00 for the first book, 50p for the second book and 30p for each additional book ordered up to a maximum charge of £3.00.
OVERSEAS & EIRE: £2.00 for the first book, £1.00 for the second book and 50p for each additional book.

Name ....

Address ....

....

....

If you would prefer to pay by credit card, please complete:
Please debit my Visa/Access/Diner's Card/American Express (delete as applicable) card no:

Signature .... Expiry Date ....